APOCALYPSE REIGN : THE AWAKENING

RUDRESH JANI

Dedicated to the kind of friends a man finds only at the
end of world - souls bound not by blood, but by fire, fear,
and the quite courage of standing together when
everything else falls apart.

Contents

Contents

Preface

The world didn't end in fire or ice. It ended in silence.

Not the silence of peace, but the kind that follows a scream too loud to sustain. Cities crumbled not just from bombs or plagues, but from the collapse of trust, the loss of meaning, the vanishing of hope. Civilization didn't fall in a day. It rotted slowly—from within.

What rose from its ashes wasn't just the undead. It was something far more dangerous: fear. Desperation. The kind of madness that turns good people into killers and survivors into something else entirely.

Apocalypse Reign: The Awakening isn't just a story of survival—it's a reckoning. A look at who we become when the rules are gone and the only law left is instinct. It's about Atlas, and the people who followed him. About what they lost. What they found. And what they became.

This isn't a tale of heroism wrapped in clean endings. This is blood on broken concrete. This is love in a world where love gets people killed. This is the story of the monster you become when you think it's the only way to protect what's left.

They say the apocalypse changes people. That it strips away the lies and shows us who we really are.

But what if what's left is something worse than what we were hiding?

This is the beginning of that question. The first descent into darkness. The first lie that maybe the monster was always there.

This is the Awakening.

—Rudresh Jani

CHAPTER I

The Light Before The Shadows

In the heart of a vibrant university town, where laughter echoed through sunlit streets and dreams danced on the wind, Atlas Gray stood at the kitchen counter, meticulously assembling his breakfast. The aroma of sizzling bacon and fresh coffee filled the air, mingling with the soft hum of morning chatter from his friends sprawled across the cluttered living room. This was their sanctuary—a small apartment that had become a home through countless late-night study sessions, spontaneous adventures, and lazy weekends spent binging on video games.

Atlas, a practical thinker and an expert in tech, moved with purpose, flipping pancakes with the precision of a seasoned chef. His deep-set blue eyes sparkled with determination, reflecting the sunlight filtering through the window. Today, as he cooked for his friends, he felt a sense of fulfillment—a rare moment of peace amid their hectic student lives. Atlas thrived on order, not just in the kitchen but in life, and cooking was his way of creating a semblance of control in their otherwise chaotic world.

"Chase, if you can't find a way to focus on anything other than your precious sci-fi novels, I swear I'll ban you from the kitchen!" Atlas called, a teasing smile tugging at the corners of his lips as he flipped a pancake in the pan.

Chase Rivers, perched on the edge of the couch with his nose buried in a book, looked up with mock indignation. His round glasses slid down his nose as he pushed them back, revealing wide brown eyes full of curiosity. "Hey, it's called multitasking! A vital skill in a zombie apocalypse, you know." His voice was calm, yet there was an underlying excitement whenever he spoke about his favorite novels. His passion for the fantastical often spilled over into their conversations, blending reality with the absurdities of fictional worlds, and today was no different.

"Multitasking or daydreaming?" Jaxon "Jax" Blaze chimed in, his mischievous grin stretching from ear to ear. The comedic heart of the group, Jax had an uncanny ability to lighten any mood. His humor was infectious, and he often took on the role of the court jester, regaling his friends with outlandish stories and playful roasts. "You know, I hear if you read too many sci-fi novels, you might start to believe you can fight off zombies with just a lightsaber."

Atlas shook his head, chuckling as he poured syrup over the golden pancake stack. "Well, if that's the case, I'm arming myself with The Art of War." His steady demeanor contrasted with Jax's lively personality, and he often played the role of the responsible leader in their dynamic friendship. His ability to keep a cool head amid chaos made him a reliable figure among his friends, a trait they all appreciated.

Max Holt, lounging on the floor with a half-eaten bag of chips, chimed in lazily, his disheveled hair framing a face that screamed nonchalance. "As long as it's not the Twilight saga. I refuse to fight zombies while holding a book about sparkly vampires." His sarcasm dripped like honey, masking a keen intelligence that he rarely revealed. Though he often presented himself as lazy and laid-back, he was surprisingly adept with firearms—a skill he never hesitated to showcase in their heated discussions about survival scenarios. "You know, guys," he added with a lazy smirk, "I've been practicing my aim on Call of Duty. I could probably take out a horde with my eyes closed."

"Sure, but video games and real life are different," Chase countered, though he smiled at Max's bravado.

"Not if you bring the same skills to the table," Max replied, leaning back. "I just need to upgrade my gear. Any zombie that gets in my way won't stand a chance."

Atlas, in the middle of assembling his breakfast masterpiece, couldn't help but admire Max's passion. "Just remember to keep it realistic. It's not like we can pause a zombie apocalypse and respawn."

The apartment was filled with the aroma of breakfast and the lively banter of friends, creating an atmosphere of warmth and comfort. It was a modest but cozy space—cluttered with gaming consoles, textbooks, and remnants of takeout containers from previous nights. Sunlight poured through the windows, casting a golden glow over the mismatched furniture, providing a stark contrast to the tension that would soon envelop their lives.

But amidst the laughter, Cade Lockwood lingered in the corner, a shadow of his usual self. He stared blankly at the wall, his expression distant and withdrawn. Unlike the others, Cade had a brooding intensity that often made him seem older than his years. His dark hair fell over his eyes, hiding the turmoil within, and his friends noticed the flicker of unease in his gaze, but for now, they chose to ignore it, believing it to be just another side effect of stress from midterms.

"Cade, you good?" Finn Ryder asked, glancing over his shoulder. Finn was the quintessential flirt of the group, his charming smile and playful banter making him the life of any gathering. He had an adventurous spirit that led him into humorous escapades, and he thrived on the thrill of the moment. "You've been awfully quiet today."

"Yeah, man. Just tired," Cade replied, his voice barely above a whisper. He forced a smile, but it didn't reach his eyes. The others exchanged glances, still unaware of the deeper struggle Cade faced as he wrestled with his thoughts.

Zane Walker, the 'cool guy' of the group, attempted to lighten the mood with a casual grin. His confidence radiated from him like sunlight, and his laid-back attitude often deflected attention from serious conversations. "Hey, if you need a caffeine boost, I've got some high-octane coffee brewing. It'll wake you up faster than a zombie on a Monday morning." He tossed a playful wink Cade's way, trying to draw him back into the conversation.

"Very funny, Zane," Cade muttered, trying to shake off the feeling of unease that had been creeping up on him.

As they continued to eat, Atlas felt a wave of gratitude wash over him. The camaraderie they shared was a sanctuary from the chaos of college life, but deep down, he couldn't shake the feeling that something was off. The world outside was filled with noise and uncertainty, but here, in their little bubble, everything felt right. They were just a group of friends navigating the trials of young adulthood, and Atlas relished these moments, even as an inexplicable tension loomed on the periphery of his mind.

After breakfast, the group decided to venture outside, where the campus was bustling with students. The sun shone brightly, and laughter floated on the air, mingling with the sounds of chatter and the distant thrum of music from nearby events. They joked and laughed as they strolled through the grounds, but the atmosphere felt heavier than usual.

As they walked past the student center, Finn spotted a group of girls laughing nearby and decided to strut his stuff. With a playful wink and an exaggerated swagger, he approached them. "Hey, ladies! Are you tired? Because you've been running through my mind all day."

The girls giggled, and Finn's infectious charm worked its magic. He loved the attention, his flirty nature shining through as he engaged them in light banter. Meanwhile, Max rolled his eyes, feigning exasperation. "Can't you just let them enjoy their coffee without your cheesy pickup lines?"

"Come on, Max," Jax interjected, laughing. "It's part of his charm. Besides, who wouldn't want to flirt with him?"

Max shrugged, a small smile breaking through his usual indifference. "As long as he doesn't scare them off, I guess it's fine."

As Finn wrapped up his conversation, the group reconvened, and they continued to stroll through the campus. The lively atmosphere offered a brief reprieve from the unease creeping in from the outside world.

Later, as they gathered in the courtyard, Atlas noticed a familiar face walking toward them. Knox Mercer, the wealthy student with an air of mystery, approached with his usual confidence. Knox was an enigma wrapped in designer clothes, a wealthy heir who carried himself with a certain nonchalance that made people curious. He had often brushed shoulders with the group, but his aloof nature kept them at a distance. Today, however, he seemed particularly serious.

"Hey, guys. I'm heading out of town for a bit," Knox announced, a hint of urgency in his voice. "I've got some things to take care of on my land. It's nothing to worry about, but I'll be gone for a while."

"Everything okay?" Atlas asked, concerned about creasing his brow.

"Yeah, just some... business," Knox replied, his gaze flicking away. "I'll be back soon, though. Just keep your heads up while I'm gone."

Zane raised an eyebrow. "What kind of business? You sure it's nothing we need to worry about?"

Knox shrugged, a vague smile crossing his lips. "Just the usual. You know how it is. You guys keep doing your thing. I'll check in when I can." With that, he turned and walked away, leaving the group in a cloud of uncertainty.

"What was that all about?" Jax mused, watching Knox's retreating figure. "Sounds like he's up to something." Atlas frowned, feeling a sense of foreboding settle over him. Knox was always shrouded in mystery, but this felt different. "Yeah, it does. But he's a good guy, it won't be that serious."

As the sun began to set, casting a warm glow over the campus, the friends returned to their apartment, laughter trailing behind them. But as they settled in for the evening, the laughter felt slightly hollow, overshadowed by an unshakable feeling of dread that loomed just out of sight. Atlas lingered for a moment, stealing a glance at Cade, who stood a few steps away, lost in thought. "Do you ever wonder how quickly everything can change?" Atlas asked, a hint of worry creeping into his voice. Cade shrugged, his expression serious. "One moment, we're living our lives like we always have, and the next, it's all gone. We could wake up tomorrow, and everything might be different—worse."

A chill ran down Atlas's spine, the weight of Cade's words sinking in. "Yeah, it's terrifying to think about," he replied quietly. "But whatever happens, we'll face it together, right?" Cade nodded, but the uncertainty in his eyes lingered. "Together, until the end. Just remember, sometimes the worst can come from the places we least expect."

As they turned to head inside, Atlas couldn't shake the feeling that tomorrow held a darkness lurking just beyond their reach, ready to upend their lives in ways they couldn't begin to fathom. The day slipped into night, and the group gathered for a late-night gaming session, banter flying as they delved into their virtual worlds. Atlas felt the weight of his responsibility grow heavier, and the bond of friendship around them felt fragile, as if it could be torn apart at any moment. Each of them, in their own way, would soon be tested. They just didn't know it yet.

CHAPTER II

Shadows of The Night

The sun peeked through the curtains, casting stripes of light across the cluttered living room. Atlas stirred awake, blinking against the warm rays spilling onto his face. A lazy Saturday morning routine awaited him, filled with laughter and absurdity. He could already hear the familiar sounds of chaos emanating from the kitchen. With a groggy smile, he pushed himself up and padded into the living room, still clad in pajamas. As he entered, he was greeted by the sight of Finn standing on a chair, precariously trying to reach a box of cereal perched on the top shelf. "I swear, if I fall and break something, I'm taking you all down with me!" Finn declared, his arms flailing for balance.

"Dude, if you fall, just make sure you land on Zane. He needs the wake-up call," Jax quipped, leaning against the counter with a mischievous grin. Zane, still half-asleep, squinted at Finn, raising an eyebrow. "What kind of breakfast tragedy is happening here?"

"I'm just trying to get some breakfast!" Finn retorted, finally managing to grab the box and holding it aloft like a trophy. "Mission accomplished!" Max ambled in, his hair a mess and a slice of pizza in hand. "That's not breakfast; that's just a crime against the culinary arts," he joked, gesturing to the pizza. "Now, that's a balanced breakfast. Good for the soul!"

Atlas chuckled as he grabbed a cup of coffee and settled on the couch. "You guys realize breakfast is supposed to be the most important meal of the day, right? It sets the tone for everything." Zane yawned loudly. "Tone? What tone?

I'm just trying to survive until lunchtime." "Survival? This isn't an apocalypse!" Jax shot back, feigning seriousness. "But if we were ever to start an apocalypse breakfast club, you'd definitely be the first to get kicked out." Finn grinned, pointing at Zane. "We could call it 'Breakfast in the Time of Zombies.' I can already see the title on the cover of a cookbook."

Max rolled his eyes dramatically. "I don't know about you guys, but if I'm eating breakfast, I want my brain food to be brain-shaped pancakes. It's all about presentation!" Finn's face lit up with excitement. "Why not make them into zombie faces? I bet they'd taste way better!" Atlas threw his head back in laughter, enjoying the lighthearted atmosphere.

Finn, desperate to change the subject, exclaimed, "Speaking of snacks, did you guys see this girl I've been crushing on?" Jax raised an eyebrow. "Oh, here we go! He's finally gonna spill the beans!"

Finn flushed, shaking his head. "Shut up! I'm just showing you guys her profile!" He pulled out his phone and displayed a picture of a girl with bright red hair and a radiant smile. "This is Alyssa. Isn't she amazing?"

Max leaned in closer, feigning interest. "She doesn't look cool at all. Your ex was still better." Jax leaned back with a teasing grin. "Come on, Finn, talk to her, channel your inner knight in shining armor! If you want to impress her, you've got to take some risks."

"Yeah, or just be yourself," Atlas added with a nod. "That's bound to win her over. Or scare her off—either way, you'll know where you stand!" Finn let out a nervous laugh. "I'm working on it! I sent her a DM, but who knows if she'll reply? I'm probably in the friend zone already!"

"Friend zone?" Jax exclaimed, pretending to be shocked. "You've got to break through those walls! You can't just sit back and hope for a miracle!"

Zane crossed his arms, leaning against the wall. "If it were me, I'd bake her cookies and serenade her with a love song. That would definitely win her over." Finn rolled his eyes, but a smile crept onto his face. "Maybe I should just send her some pizza instead. Everyone loves pizza!"

As they indulged in playful banter, Atlas couldn't shake the feeling of unease that settled in his stomach. "Where's Cade? Did he say anything about going out?" Zane shrugged, stuffing his mouth full of cereal. "Not a clue. He just vanished this morning, like a magician. One moment he was here, and the next, poof! Gone."

"Probably off on some secret mission," Jax replied, waggling his eyebrows. "You know, saving the world one errand at a time. Maybe he's off rescuing puppies or something."

"Or hunting for the legendary snack stash," Max added with a dramatic flair. "It's serious business, you know. Snacks don't just appear. You have to work for them."

Atlas laughed but couldn't shake the feeling of unease that settled in his stomach. "I hope he's okay. It's not like him to just disappear without telling anyone." Just then, the TV flickered to life again, the news anchor's voice cutting through the laughter with a sense of urgency. "In breaking news, several residents are reporting bizarre behavior in the streets, with increased sightings of what appears to be... zombies. Authorities are urging everyone to stay indoors and avoid any contact with these individuals. Further updates to follow."

Finn's face went pale as he nearly dropped his cereal. "Wait, what? Zombies? Is this a joke? I thought it was just the usual chaos!"

Zane leaned forward, suddenly awake. "Dude, do you think Cade could be involved in some sort of zombie-summoning spell?" Jax chuckled, "If he is, I hope he remembers to call us for backup! I'm not missing out on the chance to fight zombies alongside my friends!" Max chimed in with a smirk, "Yeah, but what if he gets caught up in all of this? What if he turns into a zombie?"

Chase, still watching the news, his casual demeanor fading. "Dude, if this is real, we need to figure out what's going on. We can't just ignore it."

Atlas felt his heart race. "Okay, seriously, where is Cade? This isn't like him." Finn rubbed the back of his neck, glancing around. "I still say he's fine. He probably found a stash of snacks and lost track of time."

But there was a tremor of uncertainty in his voice, and they all felt it. "If he's not back by sundown, we'll go looking," Atlas declared, trying to keep his voice steady.

As the sun began to set, the room grew quieter, the reality of Cade's absence creeping back in. Atlas glanced at the clock, the tick-tock echoing ominously in the silence. Just then, the door swung open, and Cade stepped in, looking disheveled and slightly out of breath. "Hey, guys! You won't believe what I—" He stopped short, his eyes wide, a dazed look on his face.

"What happened? You look—" Atlas began, but Cade's voice came out slurred, almost robotic. "I got... snacks," he managed to say, swaying slightly on the spot.

"Dude, you're not making any sense," Jax said, his humor replaced by concern. "Are you okay?" Finn stepped back instinctively. "What are you talking about?"

Cade's head tilted slightly, his eyes unfocused and glassy. "You should... see the snacks," he mumbled, a slight tremor in his voice. The tension in the room thickened as they exchanged worried glances. "Cade, are you sure you're alright?" Max asked, his voice laced with uncertainty.

But Cade didn't respond. Instead, he let out a low, guttural growl, the sound echoing through the room. The realization hit them like a ton of bricks, freezing them in place. "Guys... this isn't good," Atlas whispered, feeling his heart race. "Dude, what's wrong with you?" Jax asked, backing away slowly.

Cade took another step forward, his movements becoming more erratic and his gaze locked onto them with an unsettling intensity. He let out another growl, a low, guttural sound that reverberated through the air, sending chills down their spines. "What the hell is happening?" Finn gasped, eyes wide with horror.

Chaos erupted in the room, leaving behind the remnants of friendship and laughter, swallowed by the horror of their new reality. "Run!" Max shouted, pushing past Atlas and racing toward the door, but the rest stood frozen, paralyzed by disbelief.

"What do we do?" Zane whispered, his voice shaky as he took a step back. "We can't just leave him!" Jax protested, his eyes darting between Cade and the door.

"Cade, please!" Atlas shouted, desperation coating his voice. "Fight it! You can do this!" But the shadows in the corners seemed to grow, amplifying their terror as they struggled to comprehend what had just happened.

"Guys... we need to go, now!" Atlas insisted, his voice rising in urgency. Finn glanced back at Cade, who stood at the entrance, his eyes dark and menacing. "If he's infected..." Finn began, but Atlas cut him off. "There's no time for that! We need to get out!"

With a collective decision, they turned to flee, leaving behind the remnants of their friend. As they dashed toward the door, Cade let out another growl, one that echoed hauntingly, leaving a chilling reminder of the horror that had invaded their lives. Their friend was gone, replaced by something monstrous. "Go, go!" Atlas shouted, pushing everyone forward as the reality of what they were facing sank in. "We'll figure this out, but we can't stay here!"

The door slammed behind them, the sound reverberating in the silence, and as they made their escape into the fading light, the shadows grew longer, twisting with the echoes of their shattered world.

CHAPTER III

Shadows of The Loss

The sun hung low in the sky, casting long shadows over the university campus as Atlas led his friends down the narrow hallway of their apartment. The urgency of their situation propelled them forward, the fear of Cade's infection looming behind them like a dark cloud.

"Get in, quickly!" Finn shouted, already in the driver's seat of his sturdy SUV, a charcoal-gray Ford Explorer that could comfortably fit the whole group of his. The vehicle had been a source of pride for Finn—tinted windows for added privacy, spacious interiors, and enough cargo space to hold supplies they might need. It even had a roof rack where they could strap down extra gear. Atlas and the others piled in, the familiar scent of leather mingling with a hint of fresh air as they slammed the doors shut behind them.

"Go, go, go!" Chase urged, glancing nervously at the apartment complex where they had just fled. Atlas could see Finn gripping the steering wheel tightly, his knuckles white. The engine roared to life, the sound breaking through the unsettling quiet that surrounded them. Finn reversed out of the parking space, tires squealing as he navigated the chaotic streets of the campus.

As they sped away from the apartment, the world outside began to morph into a surreal nightmare. The campus, once vibrant and alive, was now filled with panicked students and faculty members trying to escape the encroaching horde of zombies. Atlas's stomach twisted at the sight of chaos spilling onto the lawns and sidewalks, the air thick with the cries of the terrified and the guttural growls of the undead.

"Turn left! The path to Block 10 is up ahead!" Atlas shouted, his voice cutting through the din of the engine and the rising panic in the car. Finn obeyed, veering left sharply as they drove past the remnants of a shattered world. A few zombies stumbled into view, their vacant eyes and twisted forms making Atlas's heart race.

"They're everywhere!" Jax yelled, his voice laced with fear as he spotted a group of zombies lurking near the main quad. "We need to hurry!"

As Finn steered the vehicle toward Block 10, a sudden wave of chaos washed over them. A cluster of zombies had gathered near the entrance, blocking their path. "Shit!" Finn slammed on the brakes, the tires screeching as he skidded to a halt just in time.

"We need to get out! We can't stay in here!" Max shouted, panic rising in his voice. The sound of banging on the windows sent chills down Atlas's spine as the zombies were drawn to the vehicle, their hands clawing at the glass.

"Get ready!" Atlas ordered, his heart pounding. "We're making a run for it!"

With a shared understanding, they all opened their doors simultaneously, sprinting toward Block 10. The moment they hit the ground, they were met with the awful reality of their surroundings. Zombies were everywhere, their groans echoing through the air.

"Right! This way!" Chase shouted, pointing toward an open entrance on the side of the building. They navigated through the chaos, ducking and dodging as they sprinted past clusters of zombies, the smell of decay overwhelming.

Suddenly, one of the creatures lunged from behind a nearby tree, its rotting hands grasping at Finn. "Watch out!"

Atlas yelled, but it was too late. The zombie collided with Finn, sending him stumbling backward.

"Get it off me!" Finn cried, struggling against the creature. In a moment of instinct, Zane charged forward, shoving the zombie away and giving Finn a chance to regain his footing. But as they fought to fend off the creature, another appeared from the shadows, drawn by the commotion.

"Back! We must keep moving!" Atlas shouted, pulling Finn to his feet. They continued to push toward Block 10, the sight of the towering structure ahead promising a momentary refuge.

As they rushed up the stairs, the weight of their escape hung heavy in the air. Atlas could feel the sting of fear and loss settle in his chest as they reached the rooftop terrace. They emerged onto the open space, the panoramic view revealing the chaos that had unfolded below.

The campus sprawled beneath them, a hellish tableau of chaos and destruction. Students ran frantically, the growls of zombies mingling with their screams. Atlas's heart sank at the sight—this was their home, now overrun with the horrors of the undead.

"We can't just stand here!" Finn said, breathless and shaken. He winced as he adjusted his position, revealing a bruise forming on his arm where the zombie had struck.

Chase, still catching his breath, looked over the edge of the terrace, his face pale. "We need a plan! The longer we stay here, the worse it's going to get!" Panic crept into his voice as he scanned the chaotic scene below.

"Chase, focus!" Zane said firmly, placing a hand on his shoulder. "We need to get to the tallest building on campus—the science tower! It's reinforced and has a good vantage point. We can plan our next steps from there."

"The science tower?" Finn echoed, glancing toward the distant structure looming over the campus. "That's a solid plan. But how do we get there? It's a trek through all this chaos!"

"We'll make a run for it," Atlas replied, his voice steady despite the turmoil around them. "We can't stay here, and we can't let fear dictate our choices."

Chase's breathing grew shallow, and he started to back away from the edge. "But what if we run into more of them? What if—"

"Chase, listen to me," Atlas interjected, moving closer to him. "I know this is scary. We've lost Cade, and we don't know what's next. But we have to stick together. If we don't take action, we'll be trapped here."

Just then, the sound of more zombies began to echo from below, their moans growing closer. "Guys, they're coming!" Jax shouted, his voice laced with urgency.

"We need to go now!" Zane insisted, determination in his eyes.

Atlas nodded, feeling the weight of their situation settle upon him. "Alright, let's make a run for the science tower! Stay close together, and whatever happens, we don't leave anyone behind!"

As they prepared to descend from the terrace, Chase took a deep breath, steeling himself. "You're right. I can do this. Let's get to the tower."

With their hearts pounding in unison, they turned and sprinted back down the stairs, urgency propelling them forward. They burst out onto the campus grounds, where the shadows lengthened with the approaching twilight.

Chaos erupted around them as they navigated through the throng of zombies. Finn, still shaken but resolute, led the charge, dodging grasping hands and stumbling bodies.

They sprinted through the campus, determination driving them onward.

As they neared the science tower, Atlas spotted a group of zombies converging ahead. "We can't go that way! We need to go left!"

But before they could alter their path, a zombie lunged out from behind a bush, and in an instant, Chase was knocked off balance. He stumbled, twisted his ankle and hit the ground hard.

"Chase!" Finn yelled, but there was no time to waste. Atlas rushed to help Chase back to his feet, but in the scuffle, the undead closed in on them.

"Go!" Chase shouted, a note of desperation creeping into his voice. "You need to make it!"

"No! We're not leaving you!" Atlas insisted, grabbing Chase's arm.

But Chase shook his head, his face set in determination. "Just go! I can handle this! I'll catch up!"

Atlas hesitated, the weight of their friendship crashing down on him. "Chase, please—"

"Now!" Chase shouted, his voice cracking with urgency. "I'll be right behind you!"

With one last desperate glance, Atlas let go, the instinct to survive taking over. He turned and sprinted alongside the others toward the science tower, the sounds of chaos fading behind them.

They burst through the entrance, the door slamming shut behind them as they took a moment to catch their breath. "What about Chase?" Finn gasped, glancing back at the closed door.

Atlas's heart ached with uncertainty, but he forced himself to focus. "He'll find a way. I believe in him."

As they moved deeper into the building, the tension lingered, heavy in the air. They reached the second floor, where large windows overlooked the campus, offering a view of the chaos below. Atlas's stomach churned as he saw figures moving amidst the mayhem, and the realization of their new reality sank in.

"Look at this place," Zane muttered, his eyes wide. "It's a fortress compared to what we just left."

Atlas nodded, trying to shake the memory of their escape from his mind. "We need to barricade the doors. And find a way to contact anyone who might be out there." But as they secured the entrance, an unsettling thought crept into Atlas's mind. What if Chase didn't make it? He glanced back toward the door, anxiety clawing at his gut. The loss of Cade still loomed heavy over them, and now they were leaving another one of their own behind.

As darkness settled over the campus, the echo of loss filled the silence between them. Atlas realized they had escaped the immediate danger, but the fight for survival had only just begun. With Chase out there, alone and vulnerable, the weight of their situation felt more daunting than ever.

CHAPTER IV

Shadows of The Past

"Mom, what's for dinner?" Chase called out, his voice echoing through the modest house he'd grown up in. He couldn't see his mother yet, but the smell of something delicious wafted from the kitchen, a comforting reminder of the consistency in his otherwise constantly shifting world.

As he ambled toward the kitchen, his mother, a petite woman with warm eyes and a patient smile, emerged with a wooden spoon in one hand and a dish towel in the other. "It's a surprise, Chase. You'll have to wait just a little longer," she replied, flashing a grin. Chase returned the smile, sliding onto a barstool by the kitchen counter, his mind wandering to the puzzles he had scattered over his desk in his room.

He'd always loved puzzles—any type, really. Crossword puzzles, sudoku, logic grids. While other kids in his class preferred sports or video games, Chase felt at home poring over problem sets and strategy games, losing himself in the possibilities they presented. He'd often imagined life as a giant puzzle itself, each day another chance to fit pieces together and search for answers.

Later that evening, his father arrived, his presence announced by the unmistakable sound of the front door clicking shut. Mr. Rivers worked at a high level in an automotive company, a job that kept him away from home for long stretches. He often returned with tales of engineering feats and corporate challenges, and Chase admired the authority and control his father seemed to command over such a complex industry.

"Dad!" Chase greeted him, eyes lighting up as he leapt up to help his father with his coat and briefcase. Mr. Rivers, tall and broad-shouldered with a face worn by years of hard work, placed a hand on Chase's shoulder. "I've missed you, kid," he said with a small smile. "Guess what? I got a chance to see one of our newest cars being tested today. The engineering team was brilliant, but they hit a few snags. I told them to approach it from a different angle, think through the problem theoretically before diving into any physical fixes." He paused, observing Chase's keen interest.

As the two sat down to dinner, Mr. Rivers leaned in with a curious smile and asked, "Alright, Chase, I've got a question for you. Who do you think is the most fearsome animal?"

Chase thought for a moment, then confidently replied, "The lion! He's the king of the jungle, after all. Everyone knows that!"

His father nodded thoughtfully. "That's true. The lion is powerful and respected. But let's think about this a little deeper. Why is the lion so fearsome?"

Chase shrugged, a bit uncertain now. "Because... well, he's strong and he rules over other animals, right?"

"True," his dad agreed, his expression patient. "But that strength is just part of the story. I'm going to ask you another question: what animal has survived for millions of years and outlasted most other creatures? Think about which animal has faced disaster after disaster, yet adapted and survived."

Chase scratched his head, frowning as he tried to think of the answer. "Maybe... the crocodile?" he guessed, but his father shook his head with a knowing smile.

"Nope," he said. "It's the shark. Sharks have been around for over 400 million years. They've survived four out of the five major extinction events that wiped out so many other species. They're not just strong; they're adaptable. That's what makes them so fearsome. They don't need to be the biggest or the loudest. They've found ways to survive by adapting to whatever changes come their way."

Chase's eyes widened, captivated by this revelation. He loved learning about animals, but this was new information to him. "But how did they adapt? I thought survival was just about being the strongest."

His father leaned forward, his eyes serious now. "It's not always about strength, Chase. It's about being able to change, to respond to whatever life throws at you. Strength is important, but adaptability... that's what helps you survive the toughest challenges. The shark doesn't try to control its environment; it learns to navigate it, to work with it. The shark doesn't panic; it responds."

Chase felt a surge of pride and determination as he absorbed his dad's words. He realized that his father wasn't just talking about animals; he was talking about life. "So you're saying... I should be like the shark?"

His father smiled. "Exactly. There will be times when things don't go the way you planned. It could be anything—school, friends, even things you can't imagine yet. But if you can adapt, if you can stay calm and respond rather than react... then you'll find a way through. That's the lesson, son."

Years later, Chase would find himself in situations that tested this lesson. He excelled in theoretical subjects, becoming the go-to guy for solving abstract problems. He'd dissect puzzles and strategies effortlessly, thriving in a world of ideas. But he struggled to translate this knowledge to action when faced with real-life situations that demanded immediate responses.

One day, in high school, a fire drill caught him off guard. As the alarm blared, his classmates rushed for the exits, but Chase found himself rooted to the spot, his mind racing yet unable to take the first step. His theoretical mind buzzed with options, scenarios, and what-ifs, but none of it translated into movement. One of his friends noticed and pulled him along, saving him from his paralysis.

Afterward, his father offered a gentle reminder. "Remember, Chase, theory is essential, but life doesn't always give us the time to plan. Sometimes, you have to trust yourself and respond, like the shark. It's okay to feel uncertain, but don't let it stop you from acting."

In his quieter moments, Chase would reflect on his father's words and the story of the shark. He wanted to be like that predator, ready to adapt to the waves of change, even if it meant stepping outside his comfort zone. And now, as he ran through the chaos of the infected-filled campus, those lessons rang truer than ever. His mind spun with scenarios, and his heartbeat thundered in his ears, but he fought the urge to freeze.

As Chase's memories faded, he was jolted back to the present, now, alone and struggling with each step, Chase fought the old panic that clawed at him, threatening to cloud his mind. He forced himself to breathe, to stay grounded in the moment. This was no puzzle he could solve from a distance—he had to survive, on his own. Somewhere in the blur of fear and adrenaline, he remembered his father's words: Adapt, trust yourself. He clenched his jaw, steeling himself, and with a final burst of resolve, he moved forward, gripping tightly to the hope that he could make it through, even if he had to do it alone.

CHAPTER V

Through The Shadows

Chase stumbled across the campus grounds, wincing with each step as his injured ankle protested. He'd left the others behind, a mix of necessity and desperation fueling his decision. His thoughts were a tangle of panic and determination, his mind scrambling for the next move. Somewhere in the depths of his memory, he'd recalled the faint outline of Block 10, the building where Finn had left the car. He knew it wasn't the smartest choice, returning to the very heart of where they'd been ambushed, but the car was his best chance of getting back to the science tower in one piece.

The sounds of the undead echoed around him, their guttural growls and shuffling steps growing louder as he neared Block 10. He pressed himself against the wall, his breaths shallow and controlled, moving carefully as he slipped around the side of the building. Every step felt like a monumental effort, his ankle screaming with each inch forward. He pushed the pain to the back of his mind, steeling himself against the wave of nausea that threatened to overtake him.

From his vantage point, he could see the cluster of zombies gathered only yards away, their heads twitching as they slowly wandered in erratic circles, searching for any sign of movement. A shiver ran down his spine, but he forced himself to steady his breathing, the shock of his isolation gnawing at the edges of his resolve. With Finn's car only a short dash away, Chase gathered himself, calculating the distance, and tensed his legs to make a break for it.

Carefully, he stepped out, hugging the shadows along the side of the building, inching forward in near silence. For some reason, the zombies didn't react. He glanced around, half expecting one to catch his movement, but they continued their slow, mechanical motions. With each step, his heart pounded harder, the adrenaline sharpening his senses. As he moved, he realized that every time he stilled and kept out of sight, the creatures seemed oblivious, as if he was invisible.

But he had no time to analyze this strange phenomenon. He focused on the next few steps, spotting Finn's car in the distance. Holding his breath, Chase quickly ducked behind a dumpster as two zombies shuffled closer. He could see their vacant eyes sweeping the area, their noses twitching as if they were trying to pick up a scent. For a moment, one of them paused directly in front of him, head tilting ever so slightly in his direction. Chase clenched his jaw, forcing himself to stay still, not daring to even blink.

As the seconds ticked by, the zombie turned and drifted away, none the wiser. A wave of relief washed over him, and he resumed his slow, steady crawl toward the car. By some stroke of luck, he managed to navigate through the scattered undead, finding a path that allowed him to keep out of their line of sight.

Finally reaching the car, Chase threw himself into the driver's seat, shutting the door as softly as he could. His hands shook as he reached for the keys, which had been left in the ignition in their hurried escape. He glanced around, eyes scanning the surrounding area, but none of the zombies seemed to notice him inside the vehicle. With a deep breath, he turned the key, wincing at the low rumble as the engine came to life. Still, the noise was mercifully muffled, and the creatures continued their aimless wandering.

Gripping the wheel, he drove with the caution of someone who knew that each passing second could mean life or death. The car rolled over the empty paths, the world outside bathed in the cold light of the approaching dawn. His mind was racing, trying to process the strange series of events. How had he managed to reach the car without attracting the attention of a single zombie? He glanced in the rearview mirror, still seeing the creatures fading into the distance.

Chase didn't have time to linger on the thought. The science tower loomed ahead, its dark silhouette piercing the early morning sky. He pushed down on the gas, coaxing the car forward as quickly as he could. As he neared, he spotted a familiar figure leaning out of the doorway—Zane had noticed him approaching and was already opening the gate.

The gate creaked open, and Zane appeared, waving him forward with an urgency that snapped him back to reality. Chase maneuvered the car into the entrance, parking just inside the gate before cutting the engine. He let out a shaky breath, resting his head against the steering wheel, the weight of exhaustion settling over him.

He sat there for a moment, catching his breath, feeling the tension drain from his body as he let the silence wash over him. When he finally lifted his head, he saw Zane motioning for him to follow. Chase pushed open the door, stepping out of the car with a wince as his injured ankle made contact with the ground. He hobbled toward the stairwell, forcing himself to keep moving despite the throbbing pain.

They made their way up the stairs in silence, Zane glancing back every few steps, his expression one of concern. Chase didn't say anything, focusing on each step, willing himself to ignore the pain. By the time they reached the above floor, the first light of dawn was beginning to break, casting a soft glow over the landscape.

Chase stepped to the edge, looking out over the campus, his eyes taking in the destruction in the soft light of morning. Buildings lay in ruin, streets littered with debris and the remnants of a world that had once been familiar. He felt a strange sense of detachment, as if the scene before him were a distant nightmare rather than his reality. But the throbbing in his ankle, the ache in his muscles, reminded him that this was all too real.

The others approached him, their voices a murmur as they asked questions, but Chase could barely register their words. His mind drifted back to the night he'd spent fighting his way back, the choices he'd made, the risks he'd taken. He was alive, but he couldn't shake the feeling that something fundamental had changed. He had ventured back into the heart of danger and returned, but at a cost he wasn't yet sure he understood.

Inside, the atmosphere was somber yet filled with a strange calmness. But something felt off, lingering at the edge of Chase's thoughts. He couldn't quite place it, some small detail that evaded him, an unsettling question he couldn't answer. He had been lucky, maybe too lucky. Yet as he looked back to the streets below, the worry faded, replaced by a sense of resolve. This world was changing, but he would adapt. They all would.

CHAPTER VI

Shadows of Sorrow

The morning sun filtered through the cracked windows of the science tower, casting soft, golden rays across the dimly lit room. Despite the gentle light, a heavy pall lingered in the air, an unshakeable sadness that seemed to cling to the very walls. The group huddled together, their faces a mixture of exhaustion and grief as they mourned the loss of Cade. The echoes of his laughter, his fierce loyalty, and the warmth of his presence felt like distant memories, overshadowed by the abrupt reality of his absence.

Chase sat on the floor, leaning against the wall, his twisted ankle propped up on a pile of jackets. He winced every time he shifted, the pain a constant reminder of the chaos that had erupted in their lives. The group had pulled together in the aftermath of the attack, but the bond they shared felt fragile now, fraying at the edges as they processed their loss. He closed his eyes, allowing the memories of Cade to wash over him like a wave—a tide of laughter, late-night strategy discussions, and the comforting presence of someone who had always been there, ready to fight for their survival.

Atlas was pacing nearby, his brow furrowed in thought. He had always been the pragmatic leader of the group, the one who made decisions with unwavering confidence. But today, he seemed lost, grappling with the weight of responsibility and the ache of grief. "We should have seen it coming," he muttered under his breath, his voice barely above a whisper. "I should have protected him."

"Don't do this, Atlas," Jax interjected, his voice strained. "We all did what we could. We can't blame ourselves for what happened." The humor that usually accompanied Jax's demeanor was absent, replaced by a somber gravity that hung in the air like a thick fog.

Finn stood at the window, staring out at the desolate campus below. The trees swayed gently in the breeze, their leaves rustling softly as if whispering secrets of the past. Outside, chaos reigned, though they remained safely ensconced within the walls of the tower. Finn's heart ached for Cade, but he found himself unable to focus on anything but the memories of his friend. "Cade wouldn't want us to dwell on this," he said finally, his voice cracking. "He'd want us to keep moving forward."

"Moving forward?" Chase echoed, his heart heavy with doubt. "How can we move forward when everything feels so shattered? It's like trying to walk on glass." The memories of Cade's final moments haunted him, a chilling reminder of the fragility of life in this new world.

Zane, who had been silent until now, finally spoke up, his voice steady but tinged with sorrow. "Cade was the strongest among us. He wouldn't want us to lose hope. He'd want us to find a way to survive." The resolve in his words ignited a flicker of determination within the group, a small light pushing back against the darkness that threatened to consume them.

As the sun climbed higher in the sky, the group took turns sharing their memories of Cade. Each story was a testament to his strength and kindness, a vivid portrayal of the person they had lost. Atlas shared how Cade had encouraged him to pursue his dreams of becoming an engineer, pushing him to think beyond the confines of their grim reality. "He believed in us," Atlas said, his voice breaking. "He believed we could do anything if we just worked together." Each memory deepened the sorrow they felt, but it also began to weave a tapestry of hope, reminding them of the resilience that Cade had inspired in each of them.

Chase listened, his heart aching with the weight of their shared grief. It was a bittersweet reminder that they had been lucky to have Cade in their lives, even for a short time. "I wish I could have done more," Chase finally said, tears stinging his eyes. "I wish I could have saved him."

"Me too," Finn replied, his voice heavy with regret. "But we have to honor him by staying alive. He wouldn't want us to give up."

"Speaking of honor," Max chimed in, breaking his silence. "Chase, how the hell did you manage to make it back to the science tower? With everything going on, it must have been a nightmare out there." Max leaned forward, curiosity glinting in his eyes, an attempt to lift the heavy mood with a distraction.

Chase glanced around at the familiar faces, each one etched with the toll of their recent experiences. "It was tough," he replied, his mind flickering back to the panic of the zombies closing in. "But... I remembered what my dad used to say. It's not just about being strong; it's about being adaptable like a shark."

Finn, seated next to Max, nodded slowly. "That makes sense. We need to keep adapting if we want to survive this. We can't just react; we need to think and plan, even in this chaos."

Jaxon looked around at the group, his eyes brightening with determination. "We can't give up. If we stick together, we'll find a way to make it through this."

The group nodded, a renewed sense of purpose building among them. With each shared thought, they felt the weight of their grief gradually lifting, replaced by a burgeoning resolve to adapt and overcome.

As they made their plans, Chase couldn't shake the lingering thoughts about his father's teachings. He wanted to embody that adaptability, to lead his friends through the chaos with the wisdom he had learned long ago.

In that moment, he realized that survival was more than just physical—it was about keeping hope alive, holding onto the bonds they had forged through the darkness. And as the sun rose higher in the sky, illuminating their faces, Chase felt a flicker of optimism in his chest, a belief that together they could navigate whatever challenges lay ahead.

CHAPTER VII

Shadows & Sunlight

The late morning sunlight glistened across the science tower's glass walls, casting warm reflections on the building's interior. It was a deceptively pleasant day, with a clear sky stretched wide above, as if nature itself was unaware of the dark plague consuming the world below. Finn leaned against the warm glass, gazing outside, lost in thought. Beside him, Max sat, a small smile on his face as he shared a moment of quiet nostalgia with his best friend.

"Remember that time we went hiking in the rain?" Finn mused, his eyes half-closed as he recalled the memory.

Max chuckled, nodding. "Yeah, I remember. We almost didn't go. It was pouring like crazy, and you kept saying we'd get struck by lightning or swept away."

Finn snorted. "I just didn't want to be electrocuted. But we waited it out. And then... just like that, the rain stopped, like it was all part of the plan."

"Our parents thought we were nuts," Max said, shaking his head. "But they still let us go because we were together. They trusted us to watch each other's backs."

Finn's smile grew, the warmth of the memory seeping through the bitter chill of their current reality. "We've been doing this forever, haven't we? Watching each other's backs."

Max glanced at his friend, a soft smile tugging at his lips. "Yeah. And we're not stopping now."

The science tower around them was an incomplete skeleton of a building. Ten floors of unfulfilled potential, with massive glass walls that gave a panoramic view of the desolate campus. The structure was finished, but the building itself was still in limbo—no electricity, no functioning generator. The floors were littered with lab equipment, unassembled furniture, and dusty workbenches waiting for the day they'd be put to use. That day would never come, of course, but it gave the group some semblance of shelter.

Across the room, Chase sauntered over to Finn, his expression mischievous. "So, how's the old Explorer holding up?" he asked, a smirk playing on his lips.

Finn rolled his eyes, crossing his arms defensively. "It's in perfect condition, thank you very much for bringing it back in one piece."

"Ah, yes," Chase drawled, feigning admiration. "The mighty Explorer. I'm shocked it hasn't just decided to get up and leave you yet, given all the times you've taken it over people. You treat it better than you treat your dates."

Max laughed, and Finn shot Chase a look of mock indignation. "You know what, Chase? That car has seen me through a lot. It's got character. It's irreplaceable."

Chase held up his hands in surrender, barely containing his grin. "Hey, don't get defensive. I'm just saying, if I ever get reincarnated as a car, I hope I have the privilege of being your Explorer. Seems like it's got a solid place in your heart."

"You just wish you had a car half as reliable," Finn retorted, sticking his tongue out.

Chase shrugged. "Fair enough. I'll give it credit for still running after everything."

Meanwhile, Atlas leaned against a glass wall on the other side of the room, eyes scanning the quiet landscape beyond. His thoughts ran in circles, each one a heavy weight pulling him deeper into the recesses of his mind. He'd lost track of the number of times he'd mentally counted the group, imagining all the ways he could keep them safe, all the ways he could fail them. A promise he'd made to himself echoed in his mind, relentless and cold.

It's up to you to keep them alive. No one else. Just you.

The world outside was cold, indifferent to their struggle. His friends—no, his brothers—depended on him, whether they knew it or not. He was the one who would have to make the hard calls, the one who would bear the weight of their survival. As he thought of the responsibility, an old wound reopened in his mind, a painful echo of words spoken by someone he had once trusted, someone he'd once thought would always be there.

"You'll never have real friends. You'll push everyone away. One day, you'll be left with nothing because as you are, no one wants to be with you."

A sudden nudge broke him from his reverie. He turned to see Jax standing beside him, concern in his eyes. "You good, Atlas? You've been staring out there like you're expecting an alien invasion or something."

Atlas forced a small smile, brushing the thoughts aside. "Yeah, I'm good. Just...thinking."

Jax raised an eyebrow, unconvinced. "Well, stop thinking so much. We need you here, not out in la-la land. We've got work to do."

Atlas nodded, grateful for the interruption. Together, he and Jax moved to secure the building's other entrances, piling up chairs, desks, and whatever else they could find to block the doors. They worked in silence, both of them aware of the weight of the task, both of them determined not to fail.

Nearby, Zane crouched beside Chase, who had taken a seat on one of the lab benches. "Let's take a look at that ankle," Zane said, unrolling a bandage from their makeshift first-aid kit.

Chase winced as Zane carefully examined the swollen joint. "Man, you're a lifesaver, Zane. I don't know what we'd do without you."

Zane shrugged, wrapping the ankle with practiced ease. "Just doing what I can. I'm no doctor, but I've got enough first-aid know-how to get you moving again. Just don't push it too hard, okay?"

Chase grinned. "I'll try to keep my superhero stunts to a minimum. Thanks, man."

Zane nodded, securing the bandage. "We've all got to pull our weight if we're going to make it. Just try not to make my job harder, yeah?"

Atlas and Jax returned, wiping their hands after sealing off the last entrance. They rejoined the group, each of them a little more aware of the fragile security they'd managed to build around themselves. For now, it was enough. For now, they had shelter, they had each other, and they had a chance.

Max glanced around at the others, his gaze eventually settling on Atlas. "So, what's the next move?"

Chase cleared his throat, glancing toward the ceiling. "I say we head up to the top floor. We'll have a better view up there, and there are fewer ways for anything to get in. Plus, if things go south, we'll have some sort of vantage point to figure out an escape plan."

Atlas considered the suggestion, nodding slowly. "That makes sense. Let's gather whatever we can carry and move upstairs. We'll set up camp there and plan our next steps."

Together, they began their ascent, each step taking them higher and farther away from the chaos below. The top floor awaited them, a new sanctuary within the glass walls, a place where they could catch their breath and prepare for whatever lay ahead.

For now, they were safe. And for now, they had hope.

CHAPTER VIII

Above The Shadows

Max stood by the glass wall, gazing out over the vast campus below. The mid-morning light filtered through the windows, casting a warm glow around them in their makeshift hideout, which they had come to call The Skylight. "Man, look at this view," he said, an unexpected hint of awe in his voice. "You can see the entire campus from up here. It's like we're on top of the world."

Jax sidled up next to him, grinning as he took in the panorama. "I'd say we have the best view in the apocalypse," he quipped. "Who needs beachfront property when you've got a 360-degree zombie wasteland?" He chuckled, nudging Max with his elbow. "Just look at this place—bet we could charge rent and call it 'luxury zombie-proof housing.'"

The others laughed, their chuckles echoing through the empty space. For a moment, the laughter felt like a balm, cutting through the oppressive weight of their situation. Atlas observed them from a few steps back, arms crossed and expression serious. He let them have their moment, but then he cleared his throat, drawing their attention.

"We need to stay focused," he said, voice firm. "I get it—this place feels safer, but we can't let our guard down. The second we start treating this like a joke is the second we end up dead."

Jax's smile faded, and the group fell silent, sobered by Atlas's words. They all knew he was right. Humor was a brief reprieve, but it wouldn't protect them. They needed to stay sharp, stay vigilant. In this world, even a moment of distraction could mean the difference between life and death.

They turned their attention back to The Skylight, inspecting the area and securing their meager belongings. The top floor had been built to accommodate a lab, with expansive windows that offered a panoramic view of the campus below. It was sparsely furnished, with a few newly untouched lab benches, chairs, and metal shelves. In one corner, they'd set up their small base, arranging sleeping bags and blankets on the floor. It wasn't much, but it was the closest thing they had to a home now.

Chase, who had been surveying the room, broke the silence. "We're going to need food and water supplies," he said, his brow furrowing.

The group exchanged glances, the reality of their situation sinking in. They knew that venturing out would be dangerous, but staying put without adequate resources wasn't an option. Atlas took a deep breath, nodding as he considered their next move.

"We'll need to make a run," he said, voice steady. "But we have to be smart about it. For now, let's figure out what we can see from up here. It'll give us an idea of what's out there."

They moved to the windows, their eyes scanning the campus below. The quad was littered with debris, and here and there, they could see figures shuffling aimlessly. As they watched, they began to pick out familiar faces—former professors, campus staff, even a few students.

Finn's expression darkened as he spotted a familiar face. "That's Professor Henderson," he said quietly, voice tinged with sadness. "I had him for psychology last semester."

The others followed his gaze, their hearts heavy as they recognized other figures from their daily lives. People who'd once been part of the normal, everyday rhythm of campus life, now reduced to hollow shells, wandering aimlessly through the ruins of their former world.

Jax shook his head, his face pale. "I used to fall asleep in their lectures, but I never wanted this. They were just... normal people, doing their jobs."

Max clenched his fists, his expression grim. "It's not fair. They didn't deserve this. No one did."

The somber moment was interrupted by movement at the edge of the quad. Finn squinted, pointing to a lone figure sprinting across the open space, a look of terror etched on his face. "Wait—isn't that Greg Wilson?"

Jax leaned forward, recognition dawning on his face. "Yeah, that's him. The campus bully. Man, he used to make my life hell."

They watched as Greg stumbled, falling to the ground. Behind him, a small horde of zombies shambled forward, their dead eyes fixed on him. The irony wasn't lost on them; Greg had spent years tormenting others, but now he was the one being hunted.

Finn let out a bitter laugh. "Looks like karma finally caught up to him."

Jax chuckled, though the sound was laced with sadness. "Guess he'll think twice about bullying people in the afterlife."

They continued watching, a mix of horror and fascination as the scene below played out. Greg tried to scramble to his feet, but the zombies closed in, their hands reaching out as they surrounded him. It was a brutal reminder of the world they now lived in, a world where justice was cruel and unrelenting.

After a moment, Atlas pulled them back, redirecting their attention to the task at hand. "We can't do anything for them," he said, his voice firm. "But we can do something for ourselves. We need to stay focused. Our priority right now is survival."

The others nodded, their expressions resolute. They knew what they had to do. The memories of their professors and classmates lingered, but they couldn't let themselves be consumed by grief. They had to keep moving forward.

As the day wore on, the group huddled together in The Skylight, discussing their options. The empty ache of hunger gnawed at their stomachs, a constant reminder of their dwindling supplies. Max glanced at Atlas, a question in his eyes. "What's the plan?" he asked, voice steady but weary.

Atlas met his gaze, his expression grim. "We need supplies, and the only place we know with food and water is back at the apartment." He took a deep breath, steeling himself for what he was about to suggest. "I think it's time Zane and I go back and gather what we can."

The others exchanged uneasy glances, the risk clear to all of them. Zane hesitated, but he nodded, his jaw set with determination. "If we go, we need to be fast. There's no telling what might be waiting for us."

Finn stepped forward, his face lined with concern. "Are you sure you have to go? We could go together, or maybe split into smaller groups."

Atlas shook his head. "If we all go, we leave this place unprotected. We need to keep a base here, somewhere safe for us to come back to. Zane and I can handle it, and if we're careful, we can make it back before dark."

Jax forced a smile, clapping Zane on the shoulder. "You two better stay out of trouble. No heroics, alright? Just grab the food and get back here in one piece."

Zane chuckled, the tension easing slightly. "Got it. No zombie hugs."

Finn stepped forward, pulling Atlas into a brief, tight hug. "Just... be careful. We need you back here. All of us."

Atlas didn't return the hug, his expression still serious. "Don't worry. We'll be back." He looked at the rest of the group, meeting each of their gazes in turn. "While we're gone, keep securing this place. We're going to need it."

With a final nod, he and Zane made their way to the door, the weight of the task ahead pressing down on them. As they stepped out into the hallway, the others watched them go, a mix of fear and hope in their eyes.

The door closed behind them, and the group settled back into The Skylight, their thoughts heavy with the knowledge of the risks their friends were facing. They knew that every second that passed brought them closer to danger, but they also knew that Atlas and Zane were their best chance. Because in a world filled with darkness, sometimes hope was all they had left.

CHAPTER IX

Whispers in The Shadows

Atlas and Zane stepped cautiously into the stairwell, the steel door of The Skylight creaking shut behind them. The silence of the abandoned building pressed in around them, and for a moment, they exchanged a glance filled with unspoken understanding. The air was thick with the knowledge of what lay ahead—both the tangible threat of the zombies and the weight of their own fears.

"Let's move," Atlas said, his voice low and steady. He led the way, his heart pounding in rhythm with the distant sounds of shuffling feet echoing from below. They made their way down the narrow staircase, every step a reminder of their precarious situation.

As they descended, Atlas mentally replayed the layout of their apartment. The memories of their life before the outbreak flooded back, warm and painful. Late-night gaming sessions, laughter echoing through the halls, the aroma of takeout mingling with the scent of worn books—those simple moments felt like lifetimes ago.

"Do you think it's clear?" Zane asked, his voice barely above a whisper as they reached the ground floor. He peered through the glass door leading outside, his eyes scanning the campus for any signs of danger.

Atlas hesitated, the tension coiling tight in his chest. "I hope so. But we have to be ready for anything." He pushed the door open slowly, the hinges creaking like a warning bell.

The world outside was a stark contrast to their memories. The campus was eerily quiet, the once-bustling paths now littered with debris and remnants of chaos. A chill ran down Atlas's spine as he stepped onto the pavement, the realization that everything had changed crashing down on him.

They moved quickly, keeping to the shadows and avoiding open areas where they could be easily spotted. As they crossed the quad, Atlas couldn't help but notice the remnants of their old life: a forgotten backpack, a shattered phone, the imprint of footprints leading into the unknown. Each item told a story—a story of survival, loss, and the desperate struggle for normalcy in a world turned upside down.

"Over there," Zane said, pointing toward their apartment building, its exterior marked with scars from the chaos. They approached cautiously, adrenaline coursing through their veins.

Inside the building, the familiar sounds of their lives were replaced by a haunting silence. Atlas led the way, his senses heightened, scanning every corner for any signs of movement. The hallway was dim, the flickering overhead lights casting ominous shadows that danced along the walls.

"Let's check the pantry first," Atlas suggested, his voice steady despite the growing unease. They made their way to the kitchen, where the scent of decay lingered, a stark reminder of what had transpired. He opened the pantry door, the hinges protesting, and sighed with relief as he saw the shelves still stocked with canned goods and dry food.

"Looks like we hit the jackpot," Zane said, his eyes lighting up as he helped Atlas gather supplies. They worked quickly, filling backpacks with whatever they could find—canned beans, pasta, rice, and a few bottles of water. It was a small victory, but it felt monumental in their current reality.

As they loaded their bags, Atlas felt a wave of gratitude wash over him. They had come so far, and in that moment, it was the promise of survival that propelled them forward.

"Let's check the fridge," Zane suggested, a note of hope in his voice. "There might be something we can salvage."

Atlas nodded, and they approached the refrigerator. With a deep breath, he opened the door, the stale air rushing out to meet them. Inside, they found a mix of rotting produce and unopened takeout containers, but something caught Atlas's eye—a large container of yogurt, still intact.

"Hey, this isn't bad!" Zane exclaimed, his enthusiasm infectious. "We could use the protein."

Atlas chuckled, surprised at how the small find lifted his spirits. "Let's take it. Anything that can give us energy is worth it right now."

They carefully packed the yogurt, sealing it tightly to avoid any spills. As they finished gathering supplies, a sudden noise pierced the stillness of the apartment—a low growl that sent chills down their spines.

"What was that?" Zane whispered, his eyes wide with fear.

Atlas motioned for silence, his heart racing. "Stay close," he ordered, his instincts kicking in. They edged toward the sound, which seemed to be coming from the living room.

As they peeked around the corner, they froze. A lone zombie stumbled through the debris, its clothes tattered and skin mottled. It was one of their former neighbors, a face Atlas recognized from the building's shared hallways. The realization sent a jolt of pain through him—this had been a person, a human being.

Zane swallowed hard, eyes wide with dread. "What do we do?" he whispered, voice barely above a breath.

"We can't let it see us," Atlas replied, gripping his baseball bat tightly. "We'll sneak past it and get to the back exit."

They edged around the wall, holding their breath as they moved silently. The zombie continued to groan, its focus lost in the echoes of its former life. Atlas's heart raced as they slipped past, the smell of decay overwhelming, but they didn't stop to think about it. They had to keep moving.

Finally, they reached the back door, and Atlas pushed it open just enough to squeeze through. They stepped outside into the cool air, relief flooding over them. But as they stepped into the alley, they paused. The sounds of chaos surrounded them—the distant moans of zombies, the sound of shuffling feet, and the undeniable reminder of how fragile their lives had become.

"Let's make a run for it," Atlas urged, adrenaline kicking in. They took off, sprinting toward the exit of the campus, their hearts pounding in unison. They couldn't afford to look back.

As they reached the edge of the campus, Atlas glanced behind them, the memories of their life before flashing like a film reel in his mind. Friends, laughter, normalcy—gone in an instant. He felt a surge of determination wash over him. They would survive. They had to.

Suddenly, a figure darted into their path, and Atlas skidded to a halt, his heart leaping into his throat. It was another student, frantic and wild-eyed, stumbling toward them. "Help!" the girl cried, panic in her voice. "They're everywhere! You have to help me!"

Before Atlas could respond, a horde of zombies emerged from the shadows behind her, their eyes fixed on the three of them with a ravenous hunger. "Run!" Atlas shouted, grabbing Zane's arm as they turned and sprinted in the opposite direction. The girl followed, her breath ragged, fear palpable in the air.

They dashed through the campus, their hearts racing as the undead closed in behind them. Atlas felt the weight of their supplies pulling him down, but he couldn't slow down—not now. They burst through a set of doors, seeking refuge in another building, their bodies colliding against the walls as they pressed into the darkness.

Inside, the hallway was dimly lit, and they paused, gasping for breath. "What do we do now?" Zane panted, his eyes wide with panic.

Atlas looked around, his mind racing. "We need to find a safe place to hide and regroup," he said, taking a deep breath. "Somewhere we can assess our supplies and make a plan."

The girl, still trembling, looked at them with desperation. "You have to help me! They'll come for me! I can't go back out there!"

Atlas's heart ached for her, but he knew they had to stay focused. "We will help you," he said firmly, "but we need to be smart about it. Stick close to us, and we'll find a way out."

They cautiously moved deeper into the building, navigating the darkened hallways. Atlas led the way, his senses alert for any signs of danger. As they reached a small room, he pushed the door open, revealing a space filled with old furniture and dusty equipment.

"Here!" he said, motioning for them to come inside. "We can barricade the door and plan our next move."

Once inside, they quickly pushed a heavy desk against the door, securing their temporary refuge. The girl leaned against the wall, her breath coming in quick gasps as she tried to calm down. Atlas glanced at her, concern etched on his face.

"Do you have a name?" he asked gently.

"Lisa," she replied, her voice trembling. "I was in class when it happened. I thought I could get to safety, but they just... they just keep coming."

"Lisa, listen to me," Atlas said, his tone steady and reassuring. "You're safe here for now. We'll figure out how to get you out of this mess. But we need to stay calm."

Zane stepped forward, trying to lighten the mood. "You know, this isn't how I pictured my college experience going. I mean, I thought about skipping class, but I never imagined running from zombies."

A flicker of a smile broke through Lisa's fear. "Yeah, I definitely didn't sign up for this."

Atlas allowed himself a small smile. It was a reminder of their shared humanity, even amidst the horror. "We'll find a way out of this," he said, his voice firm. "We always do."

They spent the next few minutes strategizing, discussing their options for getting out of the building and safely back to The Skylight. Atlas felt a renewed sense of determination as they formed their plan, the fear that had threatened to overwhelm him now fueling his resolve.

With a final deep breath, Atlas stood, looking at both Zane and Lisa. "Ready?" he asked.

They nodded, the fire of survival igniting in their eyes. Together, they would face whatever lay ahead, united in their fight for survival, a small but formidable team against the encroaching darkness.

As they positioned themselves near the door, Atlas felt a strange mix of fear and hope. They were stepping into the unknown, but as long as they faced it together, he believed they could conquer anything.

"On three," he said, holding his breath. "One... two... three!"

And with that, they burst through the door, ready to confront the shadows.

CHAPTER X

Forsaken Shadows

As the sun dipped low in the sky, casting long, creeping shadows across the campus, the group moved with caution. The fading light bathed everything in a dusky, amber glow, and the silence grew heavier with each passing minute. Atlas, Zane, and Lisa moved purposefully, retracing their path back toward the science tower. It was time to gather what they could from the familiar walls that had offered safety, even as the world outside spiraled into chaos.

They reached the tower's back entrance, a spot shielded from most of the campus, though surrounded by remnants of scattered debris and broken glass. The silence felt almost unnatural, amplified by the fact that the rest of the group, high above on the top floor, could see them faintly moving below. Zane cast a quick glance upward, wondering if the others were watching and wishing, for a moment, that they were all back up there, out of harm's way.

Atlas motioned to the entrance. "We need to be quick," he murmured. His voice was steady, his gaze hard and focused.

Lisa nodded, though her eyes darted nervously around the area. "Are you sure this is safe? We could be walking right into a trap."

"Not safe, no," Atlas replied, his tone unreadable. "But necessary."

Zane lingered at the back, scanning their surroundings. There was something unnerving about the way Atlas spoke, a hint of detachment that made his stomach twist. They were in this together, he reminded himself. But sometimes, the look in Atlas's eyes made him wonder just how far he was willing to go—and whom he was willing to sacrifice—to keep himself and the rest of them alive.

As they stepped closer to the entrance, a distant moan echoed through the air, sending a chill down Zane's spine. Atlas didn't flinch, his steps unwavering. Lisa, however, faltered, her face pale in the dimming light.

Inside the building, the atmosphere grew tense. The group above continued to watch as shadows danced across the glass walls. They could see the faint movements of their friends below, but the thickening darkness made it difficult to discern any details. Jax, trying to lighten the mood, muttered, "Well, this is like watching ants at work. Just wish I had some popcorn for this show."

"Not the time," Finn shot back, his voice tinged with worry. His gaze remained fixed on the scene below, his knuckles white as he gripped the railing.

Chase joined them, peering down at the trio near the back entrance. "It's strange," he murmured, almost to himself. "We're up here, and they're down there, and it feels like two separate worlds."

Below, Lisa's footsteps faltered again, her breath coming in shallow gasps. She was afraid—there was no hiding that now. But Atlas didn't slow down. Instead, he turned to face her, his eyes as cold and distant as the steel-gray sky. For a brief moment, she thought he might offer her some reassurance, a comforting word. But he simply gestured toward the entrance.

"We're wasting time."

Zane hesitated, stepping between them. "Atlas, maybe we should consider another way. Lisa doesn't look—" He stopped himself, not wanting to voice the fear gnawing at the back of his mind.

"Look what, Zane?" Atlas's tone was flat, devoid of emotion. "You think we have the luxury of hesitating? Of showing weakness?"

Before Zane could respond, a low growl erupted from a nearby alleyway. A small group of zombies had caught their scent, stumbling out from the shadows with their twisted, decaying forms. They moved slowly but relentlessly, their moans growing louder as they closed in on the trio.

Lisa took a shaky step back, her eyes wide with terror. "Atlas..." she whispered, desperation clear in her voice.

In an instant, Atlas pushed past Zane, grabbing Lisa by the arm and pulling her toward the entrance. But just as they reached the door, Lisa stumbled, falling to her knees with a strangled cry. She looked up at Atlas, tears streaming down her face.

"Help me... please..."

Zane watched, horrified, as Atlas stepped back, his expression hardening. He looked at Lisa as if she were already gone, his eyes void of any warmth, any trace of the man Zane had once considered a friend.

"Atlas, what are you doing?" Zane shouted, disbelief and anger twisting his features.

Without a word, Atlas turned and walked away, leaving Lisa behind as the zombies closed in on her. She reached out, her fingers grasping at empty air, her voice a desperate plea that echoed through the darkness.

"Please... don't leave me... Atlas, please..."

But Atlas didn't stop. He didn't look back. He reached the door, pulling it closed with a finality that sent a chill through Zane's veins. The sound of Lisa's cries faded as the door shut, sealing her fate.

Up above, the group watched in stunned silence. They had witnessed the brief exchange, the moment of hesitation, and then... the cold, calculated abandonment. Even Jax was silent, his usual bravado extinguished as he realized the gravity of what had just happened.

Finn's voice broke the silence, barely a whisper. "Did he... did he just leave her to die?"

Chase swallowed, his eyes wide with disbelief. "Atlas... he wouldn't. He couldn't have."

But they had all seen it. They had seen the look in his eyes, the way he had walked away without a second thought. And in that moment, a shiver ran through the group as they began to question the man they had followed, the man they had trusted to keep them safe.

Back on the ground floor, Zane struggled to contain his anger as he confronted Atlas. "How could you do that? She was begging for your help!"

Atlas met his gaze, his expression unreadable. "Let's go upstairs."

Zane was completely shocked, a mixture of disgust and sorrow etched into his features. In that moment, he saw Atlas not as a leader, not as a friend, but as something cold and unfeeling, a man willing to sacrifice anyone who got in his way.

They walked in silence, the weight of what had just transpired hanging heavy in the air. And as they returned to the tower, Zane couldn't shake the feeling that they had crossed a line, that they had lost something precious in the fading light.

The group was waiting, their faces a mixture of horror and confusion. They knew what had happened, but they needed to hear it, to understand the choices Atlas had made.

CHAPTER XI

Shadows of Betrayal

The science tower loomed against the backdrop of the deepening twilight, casting long shadows over the campus. Inside, the atmosphere was thick with tension, the echo of Lisa's death still haunting the group. Atlas stood at the center of the room, arms crossed, a stone wall amidst a sea of confusion and anger. Zane, seething, paced back and forth, his frustration palpable.

"Are you serious, Atlas?" Zane exclaimed, his voice cracking with emotion. "You just let her die! You didn't even try to help her!"

"Helping her would have put us all at risk," Atlas replied, his tone icy and devoid of warmth. "You have to understand, this is about survival. She was already too far gone—"

"Too far gone?" Zane interrupted, his voice rising. "You think that makes it okay to just shut the door on her? You watched her beg for help! What kind of monster are you?"

Max stood nearby, glancing nervously between the two, unsure whether to intervene. Finn, who had been silent until now, stepped forward, his brow furrowed. "Look, we all know things are tough, but—"

"No!" Zane snapped, turning on Finn. "You're defending him? He just abandoned someone that was surviving out there!"

Atlas's expression hardened, and for a moment, it seemed as if he might strike back. Instead, he took a deep breath, steadying himself. "She was scratched by a zombie while escaping the other block. It was only a matter of time before she turned. Helping her would have meant risking all of us, and you know it."

The room fell silent, the weight of his words settling over them like a heavy blanket. Zane opened his mouth to argue but then stopped, his anger giving way to a profound sorrow. The group exchanged glances, their expressions a mix of fear and uncertainty. Atlas's eyes darted around the room, reading the faces of his friends, now allies in a fight for survival but also witnesses to his chilling resolve.

"We can't afford to be sentimental," Atlas continued, his voice softer now but still firm. "Every decision we make must prioritize our safety. You all need to understand that."

Finn spoke next, his voice trembling slightly. "But what if we lose our humanity in the process?"

Zane nodded vigorously, encouraged by Finn's words. "Exactly! We can't let this world change who we are. We have to hold on to something—"

"What's the point of holding on to something if it gets us killed?" Atlas shot back, his frustration bubbling to the surface again. "We can't save everyone. We have to look out for ourselves. That's the reality we're in now!"

"Reality?" Zane echoed bitterly. "You mean the reality where we just let people die? Where do we abandon our own?"

A silence enveloped the room. Atlas felt the chasm widening between him and the rest of the group. He was supposed to be their leader, their protector, but now he could sense their doubt and resentment festering.

"You're all acting like I'm the villain here," Atlas said, his voice low and strained. "I'm trying to keep us alive. That's my only goal."

Zane stepped forward, eyes blazing. "Then maybe you should reconsider what that means! Because right now, you're just as much a threat to our survival as the zombies outside."

Max, unable to bear the tension, interrupted, "Okay, let's just take a breath. We're all on edge. This is hard for everyone."

Atlas glared at Max, who shrank back slightly. "No, Max. This isn't just about stress. This is about trust. If we can't trust each other, then we're already dead."

Chase, who had remained quiet, finally spoke. "We need to find a way to move forward. We can't dwell on anyone's death. We have to keep our focus."

"Focus on what?" Zane shot back. "More of Atlas's cold calculations? We can't just sit here like nothing happened!"

"Enough!" Atlas yelled, his voice reverberating off the glass walls. The group stood in tense silence, their expressions reflecting a mix of hurt and confusion. Slowly, Zane stepped back, his anger replaced with resignation. "Fine. What do we do now?"

Atlas took a moment to gather his thoughts. "We need to establish a plan. Resources are enough for now but they will not last forever, and we can't keep relying on scavenging missions without a strategy."

Zane crossed his arms, still unconvinced but willing to follow Atlas's lead—for now. "Okay, but we need to ensure that we're making decisions together. No more secrets."

"Agreed," Atlas said, relieved that at least they were starting to find common ground.

The room fell into a thoughtful silence as they considered the challenges ahead.

"Maybe we should also think about how to keep morale up," Max suggested quietly. "We can't let fear take over. We need some sense of normalcy."

"Normalcy?" Zane snorted. "In a zombie apocalypse?"

"Hey," Max said defensively. "It's about finding moments of joy. If we don't, we're going to break down completely."

Finn nodded. "Max has a point. Maybe we can designate a night for games or storytelling. Something to lift our spirits."

As they discussed plans to strengthen their survival, a flicker of hope began to return to the room. They were still a unit, still a group, despite the shadows of betrayal that lingered in their minds.

As night fell, Zane decided to take charge of preparing dinner for everyone. He moved to the makeshift kitchen area of the tower, rummaging through their dwindling supplies, while the others began to disperse, each finding their own corner to reflect on the events of the day.

Zane stirred a pot of soup over the small camping stove, the aroma wafting through the room. He worked quietly, lost in his thoughts about the argument, about Lisa, and the growing rift between him and Atlas. He couldn't shake the feeling that things were only going to get worse from here.

"Need any help?" Finn asked, stepping into the kitchen area.

"No, I've got it," Zane replied, forcing a smile. "I can manage a simple dinner."

"Okay, just let me know," Finn said, a hint of concern lacing his voice before he turned to join the others.

As Zane stirred the pot, his thoughts wandered back to Lisa. Her pleading face haunted him, her cries for help echoing in his mind. What had he been doing? He could have tried harder, could have convinced Atlas to save her. But the cold truth was that Atlas had made the choice. He had let her die and somewhere he believed that it was not his fault.

Once dinner was ready, Zane called the group together, the weight of the earlier confrontation still evident in the air. They gathered around the small table, each person finding their place as the atmosphere shifted from tense to somber.

"Here's your dinner," Zane announced, serving the soup into bowls. "It's not much, but it's what we have."

Max took a sip and nodded. "Not bad, Zane. You should be the cook from now on."

Zane offered a weak smile, but his heart wasn't in it. As they began to eat, the silence settled over them like a thick fog. The soup was warm and comforting, but it did little to alleviate the emotional turmoil each of them felt.

As they finished their meal in silence, the shadows around them deepened, and the weight of their losses loomed large. Each of them was lost in their thoughts, the echo of betrayal ringing in their minds. They were survivors in a world gone mad, but the cost of that survival was beginning to take its toll on their souls.

Finally, as the last remnants of soup were consumed, Atlas stood and cleared the table, a heaviness lingering in the air. "Let's clean up and get some rest. Tomorrow will be a new day," he said, but his voice lacked its usual conviction.

Zane nodded, still unable to shake the bitterness he felt towards Atlas. As they worked side by side, washing dishes in silence, the shadows of betrayal seemed to deepen, casting a pall over their fragile unity.

In the end, all they had left were their choices—and the shadows of betrayal that now defined their existence.

CHAPTER XII

Shadows of Memory

"Cade, you can't keep doing this!" Finn's voice rang out in the quiet of the past, a reminder of a time when laughter was abundant. They were in the university courtyard, surrounded by the vibrant hues of autumn leaves, as Finn gestured animatedly to Cade, who lounged on the grass, his trademark smirk plastered across his face.

"Relax, Finn! It's just a little fun," Cade replied nonchalantly, tossing a pebble at a nearby tree, causing a cascade of leaves to tumble down. "Besides, what's the worst that could happen?"

Finn sighed, running a hand through his messy hair. "You know what I mean. You're always pulling these pranks, and it's getting out of hand. Remember what happened with Jess? She didn't talk to you for weeks after that."

Cade shrugged, unbothered. "She just needs to lighten up. I'm just trying to have a good time, man. No one's getting hurt." But Finn could see the glimmer of mischief in his friend's eyes, the way he thrived on the adrenaline of chaos.

Jess had been Finn's girlfriend at the time, a sweet girl with a radiant smile and an infectious laugh that had captivated him.

"Look, I'm just saying, be careful, alright? Not everyone finds your humor as charming as you do," Finn replied, trying to keep his tone light.

"Aw, don't be such a buzzkill! Let's go grab a drink instead," Cade suggested, standing up and stretching. "We can hit the campus bar. Jess will get over it."

"Fine, but you owe me. If Jess finds out we were there and you did something stupid, I'm blaming you!" Finn shot back, though a small smile broke through. Cade's enthusiasm was hard to resist, even if it often led to trouble.

Finn didn't know it then, but that would be one of the last carefree moments they shared before the world descended into chaos. In the following weeks, as the outbreak began and the campus fell silent, the memory of those days haunted him, a bittersweet reminder of what they had lost.

In the present, the atmosphere inside The Skylight was heavy with the weight of unspoken fears and lingering guilt. Atlas was hunched over the generator, the low hum of machinery filling the room as he worked to restore power. With a few final adjustments, he flipped the switch, and the lights flickered to life, illuminating the space with a warm glow.

"Finally! I thought we were going to freeze to death," Max exclaimed, rubbing his hands together to stave off the lingering chill. He glanced around at the group, a grin breaking through the tension. "Thanks, Atlas! You're a lifesaver."

Atlas nodded, feeling a rush of pride mixed with the burden of leadership. He knew that every small victory was critical to maintaining morale, especially after the long, cold nights they had endured. The warmth of the lights wrapped around them, momentarily dispelling the shadows of their fears.

"Yeah, man, you really came through," Zane chimed in, his voice tinged with genuine appreciation. "I was starting to think we'd have to huddle for warmth like a bunch of penguins."

"More like a bunch of frozen zombies," Jax quipped, eliciting a few chuckles from the group. Despite their dire circumstances, moments like these reminded them of their humanity, of the friendships that had formed amidst the chaos.

As they settled into the routine of their new lives, the weight of their situation bore down heavily on them. Atlas took a deep breath, scanning the faces of his friends—no, his family. They had survived so much together, but the reality of their world was still unforgiving.

"Listen, we need to take this seriously," Atlas began, his tone shifting to one of gravity. "We can't afford to let our guard down. We've lost too much already." The laughter faded as his words hung in the air, a stark reminder of the dangers lurking outside their walls.

"Yeah, yeah, we get it, Mr. Serious," Jax replied, trying to inject some humor back into the conversation. "But can't we at least enjoy our light show for a bit? It's not every day you get to have electricity in the apocalypse!"

Chase stepped forward, shaking his head. "Jax has a point, but we can't forget why we're here. We need to learn how to protect ourselves, to fight back. This isn't a game anymore."

Atlas nodded in agreement. "Chase is right. We have to be prepared for anything. The world outside is changing, and we need to adapt if we want to survive."

"Fighting skills?" Max raised an eyebrow, clearly skeptical. "You mean like karate or something? I'm more of a lover than a fighter, you know?"

"Trust me, Max, it's not as glamorous as it sounds," Zane interjected with a smirk. "You're better off in the kitchen than in the ring."

Max shot Zane a playful glare. "I can still throw a mean punch if I have to. Just you wait!"

"Yeah, let's hope it doesn't come to that," Chase said, suppressing a smile. The banter offered a brief respite from their grim reality, a reminder of the bonds they had forged in the face of adversity.

As the conversation shifted to strategies for practicing their newfound skills, Finn's mind wandered back to Cade. He recalled how their friendship had become strained as the chaos unfolded, how he had watched Cade's carefree demeanor dissolve into desperation. The guilt gnawed at him—he could have done more, said more, been a better friend.

"Guys, I know we're all feeling the pressure, but we need to stick together," Finn said suddenly, his voice breaking the chatter. "We can't let the past tear us apart. Cade wouldn't want that."

Atlas's gaze sharpened at the mention of Cade, sensing the weight of Finn's words. "We can't forget those we lost. We need to honor them by surviving, by making sure their sacrifices mean something."

A silence fell over the group as they absorbed his words. They each reflected on the losses they had endured, the friends who had become victims of the outbreak. The memories flooded back, bittersweet and haunting.

As they sat in the warm glow of the lights, a heavy realization settled upon them. They were all haunted by the past, each carrying the scars of what they had lost. But they were also determined to keep moving forward, to learn from their mistakes and become stronger together.

With the power restored, the atmosphere began to shift, filled with a sense of hope mingled with fear. They shared stories, laughter, and even moments of silence, bonding over the shared experience of survival.

In that moment, they knew they had to prepare for the battles ahead, not just against the zombies outside, but against the darkness that threatened to consume them from within. As they finished their dinner in silence, Zane stood up and began to clear the dishes. "Well, I guess it's time to get serious, huh? Fighting skills, here we come!"

Finn smirked, trying to lighten the mood. "I can already see the headlines: 'Survivors Turned Fighting Team!'"

"Yeah, right! More like 'A Bunch of Goofballs Trying to Survive,'" Jax added, and laughter erupted again, filling the room with warmth.

Atlas watched his friends with a heavy heart, knowing that the journey ahead would not be easy, but for now, they had each other.

CHAPTER XIII

Shadows of Strength

It was a new day, the sun rising with a golden hue that broke through the remnants of the night, illuminating the science tower's glass walls. The warm rays filtered in, casting a soft glow over the makeshift training area where the group had gathered. They had been living in this new world for days now, but today marked a turning point. The realization that their survival depended on more than just luck hung heavy in the air.

Atlas stood at the front, his arms crossed and his expression serious. "Today, we begin our training. We can't just wait for the next crisis to hit. We need to be ready for anything. Strength isn't just physical; it's about resilience, mental toughness, and knowing how to protect each other."

Max, leaning against the wall with a cocky grin, piped up, "So, are we turning into superheroes or just really strong survivors? Because I've always wanted to be Batman."

Jax, standing next to him, added with a laugh, "You'll make a terrible Batman, Max. More like Robin—sidekick material at best!"

The lighthearted banter drew chuckles from the group, easing the palpable tension. Atlas couldn't help but smile, even as he maintained the seriousness of the situation. "Alright, enough joking around. This is important. We're going to focus on combat training today—how to defend ourselves against threats and work as a team."

Finn, fidgeting nervously, glanced around at his friends. "I mean, how hard can this really be? I've never been in a fight before."

"Don't worry, Finn," Jax said, clapping him on the back. "If you get in trouble, just call for us. We'll come to the rescue! Or at least laugh while you run away."

"Very comforting, Jax," Finn replied, rolling his eyes but unable to suppress a smile.

Atlas continued, "Let's pair up. I want you to push each other, test your limits, and don't hold back. If we're going to survive, we need to know we can rely on each other in any situation."

The group broke into pairs, each team taking a different section of the training area. Atlas paired off with Zane, the two of them demonstrating various combat techniques. The others began to spar, laughter and shouts mixing with the sounds of effort as they worked through the drills.

Max faced Finn, a playful glint in his eyes. "Ready to throw some punches, buddy?"

Finn laughed nervously. "I'm not sure I'm ready to punch anyone. Can't we just stick to hugs and high-fives?"

"Come on! You're not going to get strong by hugging your way through this!" Max replied, bouncing on his feet like a boxer. "Just give it your best shot, and I promise I won't cry if you accidentally hit me."

With that, they began their practice, Max leading with a light jab that Finn instinctively dodged, nearly tripping over his own feet in the process.

"See? You're already doing better than I expected!" Max teased.

"Thanks, I think," Finn said, determination seeping into his voice as he threw a clumsy punch.

Atlas and Zane trained nearby, their movements fluid and practiced. "You know," Zane said, breathing heavily, "this isn't so bad. We need to be ready, but I never thought training could be fun."

"Yeah, well, it's better than sitting around feeling helpless," Atlas replied. "We have to keep ourselves strong for the group. Each of us has a role to play, and the more capable we are, the better we can protect each other."

Atlas's words resonated with Zane as he threw a solid punch, connecting with Atlas's block. "Exactly. We need to know what we're capable of. It's all about growth."

Meanwhile, Finn was beginning to feel more at ease, his confidence growing with every light jab he threw. Max was surprisingly encouraging, and the laughter they shared lightened the weight of their grim reality, even if only for a moment.

As the sun climbed higher in the sky, the training continued. They moved on to more complex drills—defense tactics, taking down opponents, and learning to work as a cohesive unit. Chase and Jax teamed up, showcasing their own skills, and Atlas watched intently, his mind racing with ideas for the future.

After hours of training, Atlas called the group to gather around him. "Alright, everyone. Great job today! I know this is just the beginning, but I want to remind you that we're in this together. Each one of us has strengths to bring to the table. We need to support one another, not just in training but in every decision we make from now on."

The group nodded, the camaraderie strengthening as they realized the importance of their mission. As they began to wind down, Jax couldn't resist a cheeky comment. "So, when do we get to fight some zombies? I'm ready to take my skills to the streets!"

Atlas chuckled, "Let's not rush into danger just yet. We need to hone our skills first before we go out on a real mission."

As they wrapped up for the day, a sense of accomplishment filled the air. Finn felt more confident than he had in days, knowing that they were taking steps toward improving their survival chances.

Over the next three days, the group immersed themselves in an intense training regimen, transforming the makeshift area within the science tower into a vibrant hub of activity and determination. Each day began at dawn, the sun casting a warm glow as they gathered, fueled by a sense of urgency and purpose. Atlas led the sessions with unwavering focus, emphasizing the importance of both physical strength and mental resilience. They practiced various combat techniques, honing their skills in hand-to-hand fighting. Finn, once hesitant, quickly found his footing under Max's encouraging guidance, while Jax injected humor into even the most strenuous drills, easing the tension with his quick wit. As they worked together, trust grew among them, each member pushing the others to their limits, learning how to respond instinctively to danger. Between bouts of sparring and skill-building exercises, they shared moments of laughter and camaraderie, creating a bond that fortified their spirits. With every punch thrown and every defensive maneuver practiced, they transformed from a ragtag group of survivors into a united force, ready to face the looming threats of their new reality.

After each grueling training session, fatigue settled into their bones, but their spirits remained high. As the last rays of the sun dipped below the horizon on the third evening, Zane gathered the group for a quick meeting. "Guys, we can't ignore the basics—we need to talk about food and water. We're running low, and if we want to keep this training going, we have to restock."

Chase nodded, his expression serious. "We need to plan our first field mission. We should head to the grocery store near the police station. It's our best bet for supplies."

"I'm in!" Max said, bouncing with excitement. "We can finally test out our skills for real!"

Finn hesitated, anxiety creeping in again. "What if we run into zombies? I mean, it's not like we're experts or anything."

"Exactly! That's why we train!" Zane replied. "If we stick together and keep our wits about us, we can handle whatever comes our way."

"Alright, alright, I'm in," Finn relented, determination starting to spark within him. "But I'm definitely taking the rear. I'm not ready to be the hero just yet."

Atlas couldn't help but smile at the group's growing enthusiasm. "Okay, let's get organized. I want us to set out as soon as we can. Let's gather our gear, make a list of what we need, and prepare for what lies ahead."

As they began to strategize, the tension shifted from anxiety to excitement. They were taking control of their situation, preparing to face the outside world together.

After a quick planning session, Jax, Max, and Finn decided they would go together on the first field mission. "Three musketeers!" Jax exclaimed, striking a dramatic pose.

"More like three idiots going to get themselves killed," Finn muttered, but a smile crept onto his face.

The trio decided to set out next morning, ready to confront whatever challenges lay ahead, and the shadows that loomed over them seemed a little less daunting in the light of their friendship.

CHAPTER XIV

Shadows of Survival

The sun hung high in the sky, casting long shadows over the crumbling remains of the world. Finn, Max, and Jax stood at the entrance of the science tower, steeling themselves for the mission ahead. It had been three days of grueling training, and though their bodies ached, their minds were sharpened by the relentless drills Atlas had put them through. The time had come to venture beyond their temporary safe haven to gather critical supplies.

"Alright, this is it," Finn muttered nervously, his fingers twitching around the straps of his backpack. "We stick together, move fast, and stay out of sight. No mistakes."

Max, lounging against the wall, gave a half-hearted shrug. "Or we wait here, and maybe the zombies will just starve to death."

"Max," Jax said, shaking his head with a wry grin. "You and I both know that's not happening. Those things aren't slowing down any time soon."

Max sighed. "Yeah, yeah. Just thought I'd try my luck."

As they stepped into the harsh sunlight, the silence of the abandoned campus was unnerving. Every broken window and overturned car was a reminder of how the world had been ripped apart. Finn couldn't shake the uneasy feeling that they were being watched, even though the streets seemed empty.

"We should move quickly," Jax said, taking the lead. His usual carefree demeanor had been replaced by a serious focus, his sharp eyes scanning every shadow for signs of danger. Finn followed close behind, his nerves on edge, while Max trailed a few steps behind, appearing casual but keeping one hand on his baseball bat.

The walk through the city streets was slow and tense. The trio stayed close to the walls, using the wreckage of vehicles and fallen debris for cover. Finn's heart hammered in his chest with every footstep, the fear of what could be lurking just out of sight keeping him on high alert.

As they reached the edge of the campus, the trio paused to catch their breath, exchanging quick glances. The grocery store they were headed to was only a few blocks away, but that short distance felt like miles. Every street could be hiding death.

"We've got to make this quick," Finn said, his voice barely above a whisper. "In and out."

"I've got your back," Jax replied, his gaze steady. "Let's move."

They kept a brisk pace, weaving through the streets toward the grocery store. It wasn't long before they reached the shattered storefront, its windows broken and the door hanging loosely on its hinges.

Jax gestured for them to enter. "Stay close. No noise."

The store was dimly lit by slivers of sunlight that filtered through the broken windows. Shelves were overturned, and the remnants of a desperate looting spree were scattered across the floor. It smelled of decay and rot—faint but unmistakable.

Finn's hands trembled slightly as he rummaged through the aisles. "Canned food, water, anything we can carry," he whispered.

Max was already eyeing the snack aisle, but Jax shot him a warning look. "Focus, man. We're not here for a midnight snack."

"I know, I know," Max grumbled. "Just trying to lighten the mood."

Suddenly, a distant noise made them all freeze in place. It was faint at first, like the shuffle of feet on broken glass. But then it grew louder. The unmistakable, wet, hungry sound of something approaching.

Finn's stomach dropped. "We have to go."

Before anyone could respond, the sound exploded into a cacophony of snarls and shrieks. The zombies came out of nowhere—ripping through the aisles like wild animals. These weren't the shambling, clumsy creatures of old. They moved with terrifying speed, their eyes blazing with a desperate hunger. Torn flesh hung from their bones, and yet they surged forward, driven by an insatiable need to feed.

"Run!" Jax barked, his voice commanding over the chaos.

Finn didn't need to be told twice. He bolted toward the store's back exit, his heart hammering in his chest. The snarls of the undead were right behind them, claws scraping against the shelves as they tore after the group.

Max stumbled over an overturned display, nearly falling before Jax yanked him back to his feet. "Move!" Jax shouted, his voice full of urgency.

The three of them sprinted through the narrow aisles, the sound of the zombies closing in behind them. One of the creatures lunged, barely missing Max as it smashed into a shelf with enough force to send cans flying across the floor.

Finn's lungs burned as they reached the back door, bursting out into the alley behind the store. They didn't stop running until they had put several blocks between themselves and the grocery store.

"That was too close," Max panted, hands on his knees as he caught his breath. "Those things… they're getting faster."

Finn nodded, his breath coming in ragged gasps. "We need to find shelter, fast."

Jax scanned the streets, his gaze landing on the familiar structure of the police station a block away. "There. We'll hole up in the station for now."

They dashed across the street, slipping into the station through a side entrance. Inside, the air was musty, and the eerie silence was unsettling. They crept through the hallways, their footsteps echoing softly in the empty building.

"Do you think it's safe here?" Finn whispered.

Jax shrugged. "Safer than out there."

Suddenly, a noise from down the hall made them stop in their tracks. It was faint, but unmistakable—the sound of footsteps. Human footsteps.

"Who's there?" Jax called out, his voice steady but cautious.

A man and woman emerged from around the corner, their faces gaunt and weary. They looked like they had been through hell. The man, tall and lean, stepped forward, raising his hands to show he wasn't a threat.

"We're not infected," he said quickly. "We've been hiding here for days."

Finn eyed them warily. "Who are you?"

"I'm Alex," the man replied, nodding toward the woman beside him. "This is Taylor. We got separated from our group. We've been holed up in the station, trying to stay alive."

Max glanced around the station nervously. "This place isn't exactly the safest, is it?"

"It's all we've got," Taylor said, her voice quiet but resolute. "The streets are crawling with those things."

As if to confirm her words, a sudden noise erupted from the main entrance of the station—a deafening crash, followed by the unmistakable snarls of zombies. They were coming. Fast.

"We need to get out of here," Finn said, his voice tight with panic.

Jax nodded, his jaw clenched. "Let's move."

They ran deeper into the station, their footsteps echoing off the walls. The snarls and growls of the undead grew louder as the creatures stormed into the building, their hunger driving them forward with terrifying speed.

"Here!" Max shouted, pointing to a sturdy door at the end of the hall. They rushed inside, slamming it shut behind them. The door held, but the sound of the zombies clawing at the walls outside sent chills down their spines.

The room was dark, but as their eyes adjusted, Max's face lit up. Against one wall, gleaming in the faint light, was an array of guns and ammunition.

Max let out a low whistle, his voice filled with awe. "Now this is what I'm talking about. Looks like we just found ourselves a little slice of heaven."

As they caught their breath, the sounds of the zombies outside didn't relent. The dead were out there—relentless, fast, and starving for flesh.

And they would be back.

CHAPTER XV

Fire in The Shadows

The air inside the police station was thick with tension, an oppressive weight pressing down on them. The groaning of the undead outside was growing louder, more persistent. It was like they could smell the fear and desperation seeping from the cracks in the barricade. Finn, Max, and Jax stood in a dimly lit room, their shadows flickering against the walls. They were low on options, and everyone knew it.

Jax rubbed his hands together, a grin tugging at the corner of his lips. "Alright, boys, here's the plan: we set them on fire, and then... we run like hell. Sound good?"

Finn shot him a glare. "That's your plan?"

Jax shrugged, holding up a Molotov cocktail. "What can I say? I'm not just a pretty face. I've got brains too... they're just marinating in charm."

Max, who had been busy rigging up a more sophisticated defense with some scavenged supplies, rolled his eyes. "Jax, you sure your plan doesn't include trying to roast marshmallows off zombie corpses?"

"I mean, not yet—but if we live long enough, who knows?" Jax quipped. "Max, c'mon, lighten up! You've got the guns. Just keep those trigger fingers happy and we'll be fine."

Max was unfazed by Jax's banter. His focus was razor-sharp, his hands moving with practiced precision as he checked the magazines on his guns. "This isn't some weekend paintball match, Jax. These things don't go down unless you put them down hard. We need to make every shot count."

Jax's smile widened. "Oh, Max, come on. You're telling me all those Call of Duty sessions didn't prepare you for this exact scenario?"

"Funny," Max grunted, hoisting his rifle. "Let's see you make jokes when one of those things is chewing on your leg."

Jax patted Max's shoulder. "If that happens, just shoot me before they mess up my hair. It's my best feature."

Before anyone could respond, a deafening crash echoed through the hallway, the barricade giving way as the undead poured through. Their growls and shrieks were terrifying, their eyes wild with hunger. Their speed was horrifying—faster than any zombie from movies or stories. They moved with an unnatural fury, their limbs thrashing as they scrambled over each other to reach the trio.

Max didn't hesitate. "Light 'em up!" he barked, his voice carrying over the roar of the oncoming horde.

Jax tossed the first Molotov, grinning like a madman. "Catch, you ugly bastards!"

The bottle smashed against the floor in front of the charging zombies, erupting into a wall of flame. The fire spread quickly, but not quickly enough to stop the first few zombies who had already pushed through. They came at them, eyes burning with insatiable hunger, their hands clawing the air.

Max stepped forward, gun in hand. This was where he excelled. Every movement was calculated, every shot precise. His first shot took down a zombie mid-lunge, a perfect headshot that sent it sprawling. Another turned toward him, its grotesque face contorted in fury. Max pivoted smoothly, his second shot ripping through its skull with deadly accuracy.

He barely registered Jax's cheering from the side. "Look at him go! Max 'One Shot' Holt, ladies and gentlemen!"

The undead kept coming. Max fired in controlled bursts, hitting each zombie with unerring precision. His training, his experience, everything kicked in. There was no fear, no hesitation—just the calm, controlled rhythm of a master at work. Zombies fell one after another, their snarls cut off as Max's bullets found their marks.

Jax, wielding his baseball bat, swung wildly at the ones that got too close. "I don't need guns," he laughed. "Just give me a bat and a bad attitude!"

Next to him, the couple they had rescued earlier, both wielding makeshift baseball bats—were swinging with surprising ferocity. The man smashed in the skull of a zombie with a grunt of effort, while his wife jabbed at another's face, their teamwork in sync.

But the horde wasn't done yet.

Finn, standing back from the fray, was reloading when a zombie lunged at him from behind. He didn't even hear it coming—the growling was so deafening, it drowned out the stealth of this one's approach. Its clawed hand grabbed his shoulder, pulling him backward, its teeth bared and inches from his neck.

"Finn!" Jax yelled, his bat too far away to help.

Finn's heart stopped. He twisted, trying to shove the creature off, but its strength was overwhelming. The stench of its rotting breath filled his nostrils, and panic surged through him as he felt himself losing the struggle.

And then, in a flash, Max was there.

With one clean motion, Max stepped forward, driving the butt of his rifle into the zombie's skull. It staggered but didn't fall. Max wasted no time. He brought his gun up and fired point-blank into its head. The zombie dropped, lifeless, its body crumpling at Finn's feet.

Finn gasped, stumbling back. "Th-thanks..."

Max didn't even look at him, his focus still on the advancing horde. "Stay sharp, Finn. This isn't over."

The fire was raging now, and more zombies were stumbling into the flames, their bodies catching fire as they howled in agony. But even with the flames, the undead kept coming, driven by a primal hunger that refused to let up. Max, with Finn at his side, continued to take them down, every shot methodical and deadly.

The couple was still swinging their bats with surprising effectiveness, their faces grim with determination. They had fought hard to survive, and they weren't about to give up now. Together, they managed to fend off the stragglers, working in tandem with Max and Finn.

Jax, meanwhile, was still yelling insults at the zombies as he swung his bat. "Come on, is that all you've got? My grandma hits harder than you!"

"Focus, Jax!" Max called out between shots.

Jax smirked, dodging a zombie that lunged at him. "I am focusing! I'm focusing on not letting these things mess up my good looks!"

Max shook his head, firing off another round. "Maybe if you focused a little harder, we wouldn't be stuck in this mess."

Jax grinned. "Oh, come on, Max. Admit it—you're having the time of your life right now."

Max, with a rare smile creeping across his face, fired a perfect shot into another zombie's head. "Maybe I am."

The fight raged on, but slowly, the tide began to turn. The fire had thinned the horde, and Max's relentless precision had taken down the majority of the zombies that made it through. The remaining few were quickly dispatched by the others, their bats smashing skulls with brutal efficiency.

Finally, after what felt like hours, the last of the zombies fell. The flames crackled around them, the bodies of the undead reduced to charred remains. The police station was still smoldering, the air thick with the stench of burning flesh.

Max stood in the center of the room, his rifle slung over his shoulder, breathing heavily but with a satisfied look on his face. He surveyed the wreckage, his eyes gleaming with excitement.

"Now that's what I'm talking about," Max said, his voice full of exhilaration. He turned to Jax, who was leaning against his bat, panting. "You see that? That's how you take care of business."

Jax grinned, wiping sweat from his forehead. "Yeah, yeah, Mr. Action Hero. Don't get too cocky, or you'll be insufferable."

Max laughed—a deep, genuine laugh that none of them had heard in weeks. "I'm just saying," he added, still beaming, "this is the first time in a long time I've felt like we've got the upper hand. That... that felt good."

Finn, catching his breath, nodded in agreement. "I'm just glad we're still standing."

Max slung his arm over Finn's shoulder. "And I'm glad you're still in one piece, buddy. But next time, maybe don't let the zombies sneak up on you, huh?"

Finn chuckled nervously. "Yeah... I'll work on that."

Jax, his grin wide, slapped Max on the back. "Alright, soldier boy. I'll admit it—you were a badass in there."

Max smirked. "You better believe it."

As they gathered their supplies and prepared to move out, Max couldn't help but feel a surge of pride. For the first time since the outbreak, he felt like they'd not only survived—they'd won. And in this hellish new world, that was everything.

CHAPTER XVI

Shadows of Reunion

As the trio—Finn, Max, and Jax—made their way back from the police station, the silence weighed heavily on them. The excitement from finding the weapons was tempered by the reality of their situation. Max still buzzed with adrenaline, the firefight with the zombies replaying in his head, but even that couldn't mask the growing sense of unease. Jax tried to lighten the mood, throwing out sarcastic remarks about their "successful raid," but Finn barely registered any of it. His thoughts were elsewhere, churning in a whirl of memories and regrets.

The couple they had met at the station had refused to join them, too scared to leave the relative safety of the station. Finn understood, but a part of him wondered if fear would consume them in the end, the way it did so many others. He pushed those thoughts aside and focused on the road ahead, but then, something caught his attention. In the dim light, a figure staggered toward them, hunched over, clearly struggling.

At first, Finn's heart leapt into his throat, instinctively reaching for his weapon, but then a flicker of recognition sparked in his mind. The shape, the way she moved—he knew her. His heart sank as her face became clearer.

It was Jess.

His breath hitched. Jess, his ex-girlfriend—the woman he hadn't seen since the outbreak began—was alive, but she was in bad shape. Her clothes were torn, her face pale, and a deep cut ran along her arm, blood soaking into her shirt. But there was no sign of infection, just sheer exhaustion and pain.

"Jess?" Finn's voice cracked, the name barely making it past his lips.

At the sound of his voice, Jess's head snapped up, her eyes wide with disbelief. She stumbled toward him, her body trembling from the strain of running, of surviving.

"Finn..." Jess's voice was weak, but the emotion in it was overwhelming. Relief, shock, fear—all mixed into a single, breathless word.

Finn didn't hesitate. He rushed forward, catching her just as she collapsed into his arms. He could feel how fragile she was, her body shaking uncontrollably. For a moment, he couldn't find the words. All he could do was hold her, his mind reeling from the sheer impossibility of seeing her again.

"I thought... I thought you were dead," Finn whispered, his throat tightening with a wave of emotion he hadn't expected.

Jess buried her face in his chest, her fingers gripping the fabric of his jacket. "I've been running, Finn. For days. I didn't think I'd make it. I didn't think I'd ever see you again."

Finn swallowed hard, his arms tightening around her. She was safe now, but the scars—both physical and emotional—were painfully clear. Jess had fought her way through hell to survive, and seeing her like this tore at something deep inside him.

Jax, never one to let a tense moment pass without comment, walked up beside them, tapping Max on the shoulder. "Well, isn't this just straight out of a soap opera? A love lost in the apocalypse, reunited under the soft glow of a streetlight. You couldn't write this better."

Max shot him a look. "Jax, now's not the time."

"What? I'm just saying!" Jax shrugged. "It's like a rom-com, only with more zombies and fewer meet-cutes. Finn's got himself a dramatic reunion moment. All we need is some sweeping music and maybe a sunset."

Finn ignored him, his focus entirely on Jess. She looked up at him, her face streaked with dirt and tears. "I didn't know where to go, Finn. I was with some other survivors, but... it all fell apart. They're all gone now. I barely got away."

"We'll get you back to the science tower," Finn said, his voice firm. "You'll be safe there. We've got food, supplies, and... well, Jax."

Jax grinned, clearly pleased to be included. "Hey, I'm a valuable member of the team. Comic relief is important in times of crisis. Keeps everyone from losing their minds."

Jess managed a small, tired smile. "Still the same Jax, huh?"

"Guilty as charged," Jax said with a dramatic bow. "Though I must say, I didn't expect to be providing emotional support for my boy Finn's epic love story tonight. But here we are. Zombies, romance, the whole shebang."

Max, ever the pragmatist, stepped forward. "We need to get moving. Jess needs medical attention, and we don't want to stay out here any longer than we have to."

Finn nodded, still holding Jess close as they started their trek back to the science tower. Every step felt surreal. He had spent so long assuming Jess was gone, and now she was here, alive and in his arms. But the world they lived in now didn't allow for peace, not even in moments like this.

As they moved through the desolate streets, the occasional distant moan of zombies echoed around them, but Max and Jax kept a sharp eye out, taking down any that came too close. Jess limped alongside Finn, her body still weak, but her determination to keep going was clear.

"Finn..." Jess whispered after a long stretch of silence. "I didn't think I'd make it. There were so many times... I thought about you. Wondered if you were okay. I just... I don't know what to do now."

Finn's heart ached at her words. He glanced at her, his eyes soft but filled with a sense of helplessness. "You don't have to figure it out right now. Just... focus on getting better. We'll figure everything else out later."

Jess nodded, her eyes glassy with exhaustion, but she didn't argue. She leaned against him, letting him support her as they moved through the darkness.

Jax, walking slightly ahead with Max, turned back to the pair, his expression more serious for once. "You know, Finn, this is the part where you're supposed to say something cheesy. Like, 'I'll never let go' or 'You're safe with me now.' You've got to lean into the drama, man. It's the end of the world—might as well get some emotional mileage out of it."

Finn shook his head, though a small smile tugged at his lips. "Maybe I'll save the cheesy lines for later, Jax. Right now, I think she just needs to rest."

"Well, that's no fun," Jax said with a mock pout. "But I get it. Gotta keep the mystery alive. It's not a rom-com if there's not at least one heartfelt speech, though."

Max rolled his eyes. "Jax, focus. We're almost there."

The towering silhouette of the science tower loomed in the distance, a beacon of safety amidst the chaos. Finn's heart lifted slightly at the sight, knowing that once they got Jess inside, she could finally rest. But his mind was already racing with questions—what had happened to her? How had she survived this long? And what did her reappearance mean for everything they had built?

As they finally reached the entrance to the science tower, Finn glanced down at Jess, who was leaning heavily on him now, her strength fading fast. They had made it. For now, they were safe.

Max moved ahead to open the door, and as they stepped inside, Jax turned to Finn with a grin. "Well, I don't know about you guys, but I'm ready for a long, awkward reunion conversation. Finn, you better be ready for some drama."

Finn gave him a tired smile, his heart still heavy but relieved. They were back, and for now, that was enough.

As they entered the safety of the tower, the door shutting behind them, the four of them shared a brief moment of quiet. No words needed to be said—just the overwhelming sense of survival and the unspoken relief that, for tonight, they had made it through.

CHAPTER XVII

Shadows of Love

"Finn, are you seriously going to make me sit through another one of your racing shows?"

Jess laughed as she rolled her eyes, swatting him lightly with the back of her hand. They were sprawled out on the worn couch in Jess's small apartment, the smell of popcorn filling the room as the hum of a car engine roared from the TV.

Finn grinned, his arm slung casually over the back of the couch, feet propped up on the coffee table. "Come on, you know you love it. And besides, I have to show you this race. It's the one where my fav driver nailed that insane drift through the city. You won't believe it."

They were back in simpler times, long before the world fell apart. Back when their biggest worry was Finn pushing his car to its limits or Jess trying to make deadlines at her art school. The days where the apocalypse was something you only saw in movies, where zombie hordes didn't haunt your nightmares, and where love felt as straightforward as the laughter they shared.

Jess leaned back into the couch, watching Finn as he became animated, pointing at the TV screen to highlight some of the finer points of the driving techniques of various drivers. The excitement in his voice was infectious, and despite her teasing, she found herself smiling. Finn always had a way of making even the most mundane things feel larger than life.

"You're ridiculous, you know that?" she said, shaking her head. "But... I'll admit, that drift was pretty sweet."

He flashed her a playful grin. "See? I knew you'd come around."

But behind the light banter, there was something more between them, something deeper that neither had fully voiced. It had been there for months, lurking beneath their easy friendship, a shadow of unspoken feelings. Finn had always been the one Jess could count on—the friend who was steady, reliable, and always up for an adventure. But lately, the way she looked at him had changed, and she couldn't help but wonder if he felt it too.

The tension had been building for a while. Late-night talks that lingered just a little too long. The way Finn's hand would brush hers when they walked through the city. The shared glances that seemed to say more than words ever could.

Jess wasn't sure when it had started exactly. Maybe it was that night by the lake, where they had sat for hours watching the stars, talking about their futures. Or maybe it was just the slow burn of a friendship that had grown into something more over time. But now, the shadow of it loomed over every moment they spent together.

"Finn?" she asked, her voice softer now, the playful tone gone.

He glanced over at her, the grin fading slightly. "Yeah?"

"What are we doing?"

He frowned, confused. "Watching my race?"

"No," she said, shaking her head, her heart pounding in her chest. "I mean... what are we doing? You and me?"

Finn's expression shifted, and she could see the tension in his jaw as he realized where the conversation was heading. He sat up straighter, dropping his feet from the coffee table, and turned to face her fully.

"I don't know, Jess," he admitted, his voice lower, more serious. "I've been wondering the same thing."

The air between them felt heavy, like they were on the edge of something they couldn't take back. Jess swallowed, her eyes searching his face for some kind of answer. She had always been brave when it came to everything except this—except telling Finn how she really felt.

"I just... I don't want to lose you," she said finally, her voice trembling slightly. "But I can't keep pretending like this is just... like we're just friends. Not anymore."

Finn's gaze softened, and for a moment, he didn't say anything. The silence stretched, and Jess felt her heart in her throat. Maybe she had ruined it. Maybe she had read too much into things, and this would be the moment where everything fell apart.

But then Finn reached out, his hand brushing hers in that familiar way, but this time it lingered. He took her hand in his, his thumb running lightly over her knuckles.

"You won't lose me, Jess," he said quietly. "I promise you that."

And in that moment, it felt like the shadow had lifted. The weight of unspoken words was finally gone, and they were left with the truth of what they had always known: they were more than just friends. They always had been.

The weeks that followed were some of the happiest Jess could remember. They were filled with stolen kisses, late-night drives, and moments where it felt like nothing in the world could touch them. Jess had always been fiercely independent, but with Finn, she found a softness she hadn't expected. He was her anchor, the steady presence she could count on when everything else felt chaotic.

They made plans—plans to travel, to see the world, to maybe one day settle down in a place far away from the city. Finn would talk about building a life together, and Jess would laugh, but secretly, she imagined it too. They'd find a house near the coast, maybe somewhere warm, where she could paint, and he could race his cars to his heart's content.

It was perfect—until it wasn't.

Jess didn't remember exactly when things started to change. Maybe it was when Finn started spending more time with his racing crew, pulling away from her bit by bit. Maybe it was when she threw herself deeper into her art, losing herself in the world of canvases and paint to avoid the growing distance between them.

Arguments began to flare up over the smallest things. A missed date. A forgotten phone call. The little cracks that had once seemed insignificant now felt like fault lines threatening to tear them apart.

"Finn, I can't keep doing this!" Jess had shouted during one of their last arguments, her frustration spilling over. "You're never here anymore!"

"I'm doing this for us!" Finn had shot back, his voice edged with anger. "You know how important this race is to me. Why can't you just support me?"

"I do support you! But it feels like I'm the only one trying to make this work!"

Finn had stormed out that night, slamming the door behind him. Jess had stood there, feeling the sting of his absence like a physical wound. She had hoped he would come back, that they could fix it like they always had. But he hadn't. Days had turned into weeks, and before they knew it, the shadow of their relationship had overtaken everything they had once shared.

Now, sitting in the science tower with the world collapsing around them, Jess couldn't help but think back to those days. She wondered if they would have ever found their way back to each other if the apocalypse hadn't happened. Maybe the distance would have grown too great, the shadows too dark to overcome.

But here they were, together again, facing a world far more terrifying than the problems that had once driven them apart. Jess glanced over at Finn, who was deep in conversation with Max and Zane, and for a moment, she felt a flicker of hope. Maybe they could still find a way through the shadows, after all.

The world had changed, but the feelings between them hadn't. Not really. And in a world full of chaos, love was the one thing that still felt real.

CHAPTER XVIII

Shadows of the Unexcepted

In the dim, eerie glow of The Skylight room, Jess and Atlas sit side-by-side, watching the campus through a thick, silent veil. It's a rare moment of stillness, the kind they've learned to savor between chaotic runs and hushed whispers. Jess lets her gaze drift from the cracked, crumbling walls of the science tower to Atlas, noting the way he watches the grounds below with a quiet vigilance.

"You know," she says softly, breaking the silence, "back before... all of this, everyone looked up to you. Even then, it was like you carried this sense of responsibility, like you knew what people needed." She smiles, but there's a hint of sadness behind it. "Feels like that hasn't changed."

Atlas barely glances her way, his face impassive. He gives her a curt nod, acknowledging her words, but there's a tightness around his eyes, as if her comment has touched something buried. Jess hesitates, then presses on.

"Did you ever... I mean, what happened with her? I remember you two being close."

Atlas stiffens, a momentary shadow flickering across his face. His gaze sharpens, his tone shifting as he quickly changes the subject. "We should keep an eye on the main entrance. Zane set up a camera down there while Finn, Jax, and Max were out. Just in case anyone—or anything—comes by."

The conversation lingers between them, but Jess doesn't push further. She's learned when to let go, knowing that his past is something Atlas guards fiercely. For him, keeping the group together is everything, and anything outside of that is secondary. The silence that follows feels different now, filled with something unsaid.

Later that afternoon, the entire group gathers around the supplies they've stockpiled, and Max proudly displays the firearms and ammunition he and the others recovered from the police station. He stands with his hands on his hips, surveying the small armory like a general before a battle. Rifles, handguns, and a modest pile of ammunition are spread out before them, glinting faintly in the waning light.

"Now this is what I call a score," Max says with a grin, picking up a sleek handgun and twirling it once before tucking it into his belt.

Jax, ever the humorist, nudges Chase with an exaggerated wink. "Look at this, Chase. Now you don't have to fight off zombies with your endless lectures about theoretical physics. I bet they'd prefer to be shot than hear about your philosophy of adaptability."

The group bursts into laughter, Chase rolling his eyes good-naturedly as he tries not to grin. The brief moment of levity feels like a much-needed reprieve from the weight of survival that has been resting on their shoulders. Even Atlas, usually so guarded, allows himself a rare smile as Jax continues, giving Chase a friendly elbow jab.

"Come on, Chase, let's be real—'adapt or die' is probably the best line to start a zombie monologue. You've got it all covered."

Finn chuckles and claps Chase on the back. "Who knows, Jax? Maybe we'll need a pep talk on the fly when we're outnumbered. And Chase here will save us all with his inspiring words."

The laughter trails off, but a certain camaraderie remains, settling over the group like a warm blanket. Max takes the lead in organizing the weapons, distributing them based on each person's skill level and comfort. Atlas assigns himself a rifle, Jess takes a handgun, and Jax, of course, opts for the one with the most "personality," a slightly battered pistol with a chipped handle that he dubs "Old Faithful."

As night begins to fall, a loud banging echoes up from the main entrance below. The group jolts, immediately alert, and they gather around the small monitor hooked to the camera Zane had rigged up while the others were out. The camera's grainy image shows a group of survivors clustered at the main door, some banging with desperation, others shouting and waving.

Atlas peers at the monitor, his jaw tight. "More survivors," he mutters, exchanging a quick glance with Zane and Finn.

Zane tilts his head, eyes narrowed as he studies the screen. "Looks like they're in pretty bad shape. Could be useful allies... if we can trust them."

Atlas, Zane, and Finn exchange a wordless agreement before heading down toward the main door, leaving the rest to keep watch from the skylight. The walk down the winding stairs is silent, tension building with each step.

Atlas grips his rifle tightly, Zane walks with calculated ease, and Jess, who joined last second, trails behind Finn, her expression a mix of caution and curiosity. As they reach the doorway, they can hear the faint murmur of voices and the desperate pounding of fists against metal.

Atlas unlocks the door and pulls it open just enough to get a better look, eyes sweeping over the group. His gaze stops abruptly when he sees two familiar faces at the front—Alex and Taylor, the couple from the police station. Jess's eyes widened, her hand flying to her mouth in shock. She can barely stammer, "Alex? Taylor?"

CHAPTER XIX

Shadows of Suspicion

The following morning, the group gathered in a loose circle at The Skylight, with an uneasy quiet settling over them. Alex and Taylor, the new additions to their fold, had spent their first night in relative silence, careful not to disturb the established order. Yet, the unspoken questions hung in the air.

Jess broke the silence, casually talking to Atlas about Alex and Taylor, her tone light. "They seem good, don't they? You can tell they're strong. They've survived this long, and they're not exactly strangers to me. We've been through a lot together before all this."

Atlas's expression stayed neutral, a hint of reservation in his eyes. "I get it, Jess, but people change in times like these. Trusting someone just because we used to know them isn't a luxury we have anymore." His gaze hardened. "We can't afford to take chances."

Jess paused, clearly considering his words, but before she could respond, Finn joined in, sensing the tension. "Atlas, we trust you, and we always have, but Jess knows them," Finn said, his tone cautious but resolute. "They saved her life. Don't you think that's worth something?"

"Trust is all well and good until it gets us killed," Atlas replied coolly, arms crossed defensively. He glanced over at Zane, who had been unusually quiet but was now watching him with a smoldering intensity.

Zane finally spoke up, his voice laced with irritation. "Maybe you're the one holding everyone back, Atlas. You keep talking about safety, but look around—none of us would have survived this far if we hadn't learned to trust a little, to rely on each other." He leaned forward, his gaze challenging. "At some point, you have to stop questioning everyone."

Atlas met his stare head-on, his voice sharpening. "Is that really how you feel, Zane? Trust blindly because it's convenient? This isn't just about today. We're dealing with more than just survival out here."

Finn, caught between the two, glanced back and forth, visibly frustrated. "Look, I get it. Both of you are right in different ways. But we're on the edge here—if we're constantly turning on each other, what good is anything we do?"

Jess stepped closer, adding a gentler tone to the tense air. "I get that you don't trust easily, Atlas. But they saved me. That has to count for something."

Atlas's resolve wavered, her words reminding him of past bonds broken, of that haunting phrase from someone close, warning him he'd end up alone. It hurt, but he kept his voice steady, though noticeably quieter. "It's not about not trusting anyone; it's about protecting all of us. I've seen what happens when trust is taken for granted."

The tension thickened as Zane, with a final, frustrated look, stood up and walked to the other side of the room. Finn, too, seemed unsettled, muttering something under his breath as he distanced himself from the conversation. Jess watched Atlas's expression, a faint concern in her eyes.

Hours passed, each of them drifting off to their routines, but the unspoken conflict lingered. Atlas stayed near the camera feed Zane had adjusted, watching it intently, alert to any sign of movement. He knew he'd need to make a decision soon, something to address the growing tension.

As night fell, the sounds of their breathing settled into a rhythmic stillness. But Atlas's mind was a storm, churning over the question of what was best for the group.

And as the last light faded, he spoke to himself in a low murmur, "I have to do something now."

CHAPTER XX

Secrets in The Shadows

Atlas stood in the common area on The Skylight floor of the science tower, the atmosphere thick with unspoken tension. The dim light cast shadows on the walls, enhancing the sense of unease that lingered in the air. His mind raced as he reflected on the unexpected arrival of Alex and Taylor, who had previously refused to leave the police station out of fear. Now, they were here, and he couldn't shake the feeling that something was off.

As he paced, Chase noticed the deep furrow in Atlas's brow and decided to approach him. "Hey, man, you alright?" he asked, leaning against the wall.

Atlas stopped, glancing at Chase. "Not really. I need to talk to Alex and Taylor. I don't understand how they got here after saying they were too scared to leave."

Chase crossed his arms, his expression thoughtful. "Maybe they had a change of heart? Or maybe they found some strength we didn't see before."

"Or maybe they're hiding something," Atlas countered, his tone clipped. "They could have brought danger with them. We can't afford to let our guard down."

"Look, Atlas," Chase said, his voice steady but firm. "We need to give them a chance. We all have our fears, but sometimes you have to take risks to survive. They're here now, and that has to mean something."

"Does it?" Atlas shot back, frustration evident in his tone. "We're talking about our lives here, Chase."

Before Chase could respond, the door swung open, revealing Alex and Taylor. They both looked slightly out of breath, a mix of relief and apprehension on their faces. Atlas felt a knot tighten in his stomach as he prepared to confront them.

"Hey, we were just talking about you," Chase said, forcing a smile, but Atlas could see the worry etched on his face.

Atlas's gaze hardened. "You didn't want to come with us from the police station. Why now? What's changed?"

Taylor glanced at Alex before looking back at Atlas. "We realized that staying in one place was too dangerous. We needed to find safety, and we heard your distress call on the radio. We couldn't ignore it."

"But you were scared," Atlas pressed, crossing his arms defensively. "What's different now?"

"We had a chance to meet Connor and Elias," Alex explained. "They're experienced and have helped us navigate through some tight spots. We wouldn't have made it here without them."

"Where are they now?" Atlas demanded, his tone unwavering. "And what makes you think they're trustworthy?"

"They'll be here soon," Taylor replied, her voice steady but tinged with anxiety. "They were gathering supplies while we made our way here. They know this area well and can help us, Atlas."

Atlas stared at them, feeling the weight of their words but struggling to fully trust them. "And if they're not what they seem? You could have led danger right to our door."

"We're not trying to put you at risk," Alex defended, his tone earnest. "We just want to survive like everyone else here."

"Trust doesn't come easy in this world," Atlas said, his voice low. "I need to know who they are before we bring them into our home."

Chase stepped in, sensing the rising tension. "Atlas, maybe we should at least give them a chance to explain themselves. We can't keep shutting people out. We need to build alliances."

Atlas shook his head, his frustration bubbling to the surface. "This isn't just about alliances, Chase. It's about safety. I don't want to endanger the people here because we're feeling generous."

Alex's expression hardened. "We're not the enemy, Atlas. We're just trying to find our place, same as you."

"Maybe you should have thought of that before refusing to leave the police station," Atlas snapped.

"Enough!" Taylor interjected, her voice rising above theirs. "This isn't helping anyone. We came here because we believed it was safe, and now you're treating us like we're the problem."

Atlas took a deep breath, realizing the argument was spiraling. "I just need to know more. I'm not trying to be difficult, but we have to be smart about this."

As the argument began to wane, a heavy silence enveloped The Skylight floor of the science tower. The group was still reeling from the confrontation, and tension hung thick in the air like a dense fog. Max, feeling the weight of the moment pressing down on them, decided it was time to clear his mind.

"Alright, I need to blow off some steam," he announced, a casual tone masking the unease that lingered in the room. "I'm going to head up to the terrace for some sniping practice. Nothing like some fresh air and a clear shot to release some tension, right?"

Atlas, still deep in thought about the earlier confrontation, barely acknowledged him. Chase nodded, recognizing that everyone needed their own way of coping with the stress. Max made his way to the door leading to the terrace, a sense of purpose in his stride.

He pushed the door open and stepped out, the cold wind immediately hitting him like a slap in the face. The sun hung low in the sky, casting long shadows across the ground, but Max barely noticed. He was focused, adjusting his makeshift sniper position along the edge of the terrace. It was an opportunity for him to practice his aim, an essential skill in their new reality.

As he leaned over the ledge, a sense of calm washed over him. He took a deep breath, letting the chill air fill his lungs. With the world laid out before him, he could see the expanse of the campus, the remnants of civilization now turned into a haunting landscape. But something felt off, a shift in the atmosphere that sent a shiver down his spine.

Max lined up his imaginary target, his fingers curling around the air where his rifle would rest. He was about to squeeze the trigger when a movement caught his eye in the distance. Something unnatural, something that didn't belong. He squinted, trying to focus, but the shadows played tricks on him.

He leaned in closer, peering into the distance, his heart starting to race. The shapes shifted, darting between the ruins of the university buildings, their movements jerky and erratic. A surge of adrenaline coursed through him as he realized that these weren't just shadows; they were figures—zombies, or worse.

Just as the realization struck him, a noise erupted from behind him. A guttural sound, followed by a series of loud thuds, echoed from the door to the terrace, reverberating against the walls. Max froze, heart pounding as the world around him shifted back into focus. He turned abruptly, panic creeping in as he shouted, "Guys! You need to see this!"

The urgency in his voice sliced through the air like a knife, causing the others to exchange wary glances. They hadn't expected such a sudden outburst, especially after the previous confrontation.

"What is it, Max?" Atlas called out, stepping closer to the door.

Max's eyes widened, the shock evident on his face. "You have to come see for yourselves!" His voice cracked with a mix of fear and disbelief.

Atlas exchanged a quick look with Jax, who nodded. They knew they had to investigate. The air was thick with tension, every heartbeat echoing in their ears. As they approached the terrace door, a sense of dread washed over them, the shadows around them feeling more menacing than before.

"Let's go," Atlas said, his voice steady despite the chaos swirling in his mind. The group braced themselves, aware that whatever awaited them on the terrace could change everything. As they stepped through the door, Max's shocked yell still reverberated in their ears, setting the stage for the mystery that lay ahead.

CHAPTER XXI

Shadows of Air

Max stepped onto the terrace, the heavy door creaking open as he squinted against the bright afternoon sun. He had wanted a moment away from the tension inside the science tower, a chance to clear his mind and practice his shooting. But the instant he emerged, his breath caught in his throat, and all thoughts of sniping flew from his mind. There, silhouetted against the blue sky, was a helicopter—its rotors still and silent, casting a long shadow across the concrete surface.

The machine loomed large, an imposing figure that felt almost surreal amidst the desolation surrounding them. It was an aircraft of war, rugged and built for survival, with a matte black exterior that had weathered the elements. The paint was chipped in places, revealing hints of the metallic surface beneath, while the windows were darkened, obscuring any view of what lay inside. The sight sent a thrill of adrenaline coursing through Max's veins.

"Hey! Guys! You need to see this!" he shouted, his voice echoing back into the tower, the excitement bubbling in his chest.

Moments later, Atlas and Jax appeared, their eyes wide with disbelief as they joined him on the terrace. Atlas, usually the voice of caution, couldn't help the grin that spread across his face. "What the hell? Where did that come from?" he exclaimed, his gaze fixed on the helicopter.

"I don't know, but it looks like it's in one piece!" Max replied, his enthusiasm infectious. Jax nudged Atlas with a playful elbow, his eyes gleaming with mischief.

"Imagine all the gear we could find in there! It could be a treasure trove!" Jax added, his voice dripping with excitement.

Atlas shook his head, trying to temper their enthusiasm with a note of caution. "We don't know if it's safe. It could be rigged or attract zombies," he warned, but even he couldn't suppress the rush of hope welling up inside him. The prospect of a functioning helicopter offered a glimmer of possibility in their bleak reality—a way to escape, to find help, or perhaps even a safe haven.

Max stepped closer to the edge of the terrace, peering down at the helicopter with a mix of awe and curiosity. "What if it's still operational?" he mused, his mind racing with potential scenarios. "We could use it to scout the area or even escape from this tower."

As they contemplated their next move, the air around them crackled with possibilities, and for a moment, the looming threat of the apocalypse faded into the background, overshadowed by the potential of what lay before them.

Atlas, still staring at the helicopter, felt a surge of determination. "We need to figure out how to fly this thing," he declared, his voice steady and resolute. "If it's operational, it could be our ticket out of here—or at least a way to scout for resources and survivors."

Jax nodded vigorously, a grin spreading across his face. "Right? I mean, how hard could it be? It's just like a giant flying car, right?" His playful attitude cut through the tension, and Atlas couldn't help but chuckle.

"Sure, a flying car with a whole lot more complicated controls and a higher risk of crashing," Atlas replied, shaking his head in mock disapproval. But even as he said it, excitement bubbled within him. "We'll need to find manuals or something. Maybe even get a pilot on board if we can. But we can start by looking for flight controls inside."

Jax, who had been contemplating the helicopter's potential, added, "I could check the cockpit. If I can figure out how the controls work, we might have a chance."

"Good idea," Atlas said. "Let's keep the door locked and make sure we don't attract any unwanted attention."

While they formulated their plans for the helicopter, the rest of the group decided it was time to resume their training program. The urgency of their situation reminded them that while hope was a powerful motivator, survival skills were their best bet against the constant threat of the undead.

"Alright, team!" Finn called out, clapping his hands to gather everyone's attention. "We've got some serious work to do if we want to stay alive. Let's resume our training—focus on weapon handling, stealth movements, and working as a team."

The others nodded, fueled by a sense of purpose. Max took the lead on weapon handling, grabbing the firearms he had scavenged from the police station. "We're lucky to have these," he said, holding a rifle aloft. "Remember, it's not just about shooting; it's about aiming accurately under pressure."

As the group gathered around, Max began demonstrating the proper stance and grip, emphasizing the importance of stability and control. The others watched closely, eager to learn and practice. Each member took turns firing at makeshift targets they had set up, ensuring they could hit their marks even in a high-stress situation.

Laughter occasionally broke through the seriousness of the exercise, especially when Jax tripped over a stray wooden plank and fell dramatically to the ground, claiming he had been attacked by a "super zombie."

"Good job, Jax! Really selling that act!" Chase laughed, and soon everyone joined in, the camaraderie lifting their spirits amidst the looming danger.

As the day wore on, the combination of excitement and training began to instill a renewed sense of confidence in the group. They worked diligently, knowing that their survival depended on honing their skills.

After a rigorous training session, Atlas and Jax returned to the helicopter, their minds racing with possibilities. They peered inside the cockpit, discussing what tools they might need and how they could begin learning to fly. They were determined to take advantage of the unexpected opportunity that lay before them.

"We'll figure this out," Atlas said, his gaze fixed on the controls. "We have to."

CHAPTER XXII

Knock of The Shadows

Finn leaned against the wall, lost in thought as he gazed out at the darkening landscape beyond the science tower. His mind drifted, lingering on the image of his old car parked a few floors below. Ever since they'd narrowly escaped the police station, he couldn't shake the feeling that they needed something more—a true vehicle of survival, something powerful and fortified, capable of getting them through any roadblock or horde of zombies that might come their way.

With a sudden spark of inspiration, he turned to Zane and Jess, who were setting up their makeshift workstation nearby. "You know what we need?" he said, voice alight with excitement. "We need to upgrade my car. Turn it into something like...like in Mad Max!"

Zane raised an eyebrow, intrigued. "Are you serious?"

"Completely serious," Finn replied, animated. "Imagine it—reinforced bumpers, maybe some metal plating along the sides. We could rig up some spikes on the wheels or something to tear through anything that gets too close. A few steel bars across the windshield to keep it safe. This thing could be unstoppable!"

Jess chuckled, though her eyes lit up at the idea. "And how do you plan on pulling that off in a university science tower, Finn? You've seen the tools we've got. It's not exactly a garage."

"Yeah, but we've got to think big," Finn replied, unfazed. "If we're going to make any long trips out of here or if things get worse, we need to be ready. And let's face it, the car's already sturdy, but right now, it's nothing more than a getaway vehicle. We could turn it into a fortress on wheels!"

Zane rubbed his chin thoughtfully. "It's not impossible," he said, mulling over the idea. "If we scavenge the right parts—maybe from some of the junked cars we've seen nearby. We could pull off at least some of it. Reinforcing the body shouldn't be too hard, and if we can find some old scrap metal..."

"Exactly!" Finn grinned, excitement spreading. "We can build it up piece by piece. A real survival rig. I know it sounds crazy, but I'd rather have that than just sit here hoping things don't go south."

Jess tilted her head, considering. "I'll admit, it's not the worst idea. Better than sitting around, that's for sure. Plus, if we're going to start making trips out of here, we could use a bit of armor. Who knows what we might run into."

Finn nodded, enthusiasm renewed. "So, what do you say, Zane? We go down there tomorrow, check out what we have, and start figuring out what we need?"

Zane smirked, catching Finn's excitement. "Alright, Mad Max. Let's see what we can do."

With a plan beginning to take shape, Finn could almost picture it: a car armored to the hilt, a machine that wouldn't just carry them from one place to another but would protect them from the dangers outside. His mind raced with possibilities, his hands itching to start working on the vehicle that could mean survival for all of them. The ideas were endless—a reinforced front grill, metal plates for the windows, spikes on the wheels. Something worthy of the apocalypse.

As Finn talked through his plans with Zane and Jess, the rest of the group found their way up to the rooftop for some air. Chase leaned against the railing, his gaze distant as he stared into the horizon. Shadows deepened as dusk set in, casting long fingers across the landscape, a reminder of the creeping danger that lay beyond their makeshift fortress.

Jax stood beside him, unusually quiet for once, the usual spark of humor in his eyes replaced by something softer, almost melancholic. He nudged Chase gently, breaking the silence. "What's on your mind, man?"

Chase shifted, his gaze lingering on the horizon as shadows from the setting sun stretched across the campus below. "Just thinking about Knox. Wondering where he is…if he's okay." His voice held a rare hint of vulnerability, the kind he usually kept buried under layers of sarcasm and practicality. But here, at the edge of their world, the worry slipped through.

"In another time, another world…Knox would be here, probably taking the lead on everything." He chuckled softly. "The guy would've turned this rooftop into a fortress and had half the city mapped out by now, you know?"

Jax's expression softened, a faint smile tugging at his lips. "Yeah, that sounds like him." He paused, letting the silence settle between them before speaking again. "Remember that time he woke us up in the middle of the night looking for snacks?" Jax's smile grew, eyes crinkling with the memory. "You were practically unconscious, and he just kept nudging you until you handed over whatever you had on hand. He scarfed it down right there and then passed out on the floor like nothing happened."

Chase laughed, the memory lifting his spirits. "And the next morning, he told us he had the most realistic dream about raiding a grocery store, like he didn't just clean out our whole stash right there."

Jax chuckled. "Yeah, and we all just went along with it. It was classic Knox...made everything feel a little more normal, even if it meant waking up starving because he'd eaten everything." His gaze grew distant, touched with that same bittersweet nostalgia. "He was like the kid of the group in some ways. Needed looking after, but somehow he kept all of us together."

Chase nodded, the warmth of the memory pushing away some of the dark thoughts lingering at the edges of his mind. "If he's out there somewhere, I hope he's safe. And I hope he found some sense of normal...or at least something close enough."

The two friends fell quiet, letting the memory settle around them. In the fading light, it felt like Knox was still there, sharing in the familiar silence.

As evening descended, the group made their way up to The Skylight. The sky was tinged with shades of amber and crimson, casting a soft, warm glow through the windows as the world outside fell into shadows. They settled around in a loose circle, quietly absorbing the peace of the moment. The rooftop had become a space for them to unwind, a sanctuary away from the tense reality of survival.

Finn leaned back, his eyes half-closed as he took in the view. "You know," he muttered, "it's almost nice up here. Like...if we didn't have zombies down there, this would actually be peaceful."

Jax laughed softly. "Only you would find comfort in the end of the world, Finn."

The group shared a brief, light-hearted chuckle, but their laughter was cut short when Zane, who'd been idly glancing at the monitor connected to the tower's security cameras, froze. He squinted at the screen, his posture instantly tense. "Uh...guys? We've got movement at the main door."

Everyone shifted, peering over Zane's shoulder at the monitor. The camera feed showed two figures standing just outside the main entrance of the tower, silhouetted against the dimming sky. They appeared cautious, glancing around nervously, as if they knew someone might be watching but weren't sure where to look.

Alex and Taylor exchanged uneasy glances. Alex spoke first, his voice low, almost cautious. "Those two... they're the ones we mentioned before. Connor and Elias."

As the group watched, the two figures on the monitor shuffled closer to the main door, their faces partially illuminated by the fading light. One of them raised a hand, as if reaching out.

And then, a loud, echoing knock reverberated through the microphone feed from the camera, filling the quiet of The Skylight. The sound seemed to linger, spreading through the tower's silence with a strange, almost eerie resonance.

Everyone exchanged wary glances, the tension hanging heavy in the air. The night was closing in, shadows deepening around them, and the knocking felt like a signal—a reminder that, even in their refuge, they weren't as alone as they thought.

CHAPTER XXIII

Shadows of the Unknown

The knocking came again, this time louder, more insistent, reverberating through the silence of the tower. The sound felt almost too deliberate, too purposeful, echoing through the stillness with an eerie finality. It was the kind of knock that didn't belong in this world—rude, confident, and demanding attention. With every passing second, the echo of the knock seemed to grow heavier, as if the world outside was pushing in, reminding them that they weren't as safe as they wanted to believe.

Atlas glanced at the others, his eyes narrowing. He could feel the weight of their gaze on him, waiting for him to make the decision. Slowly, he rose from his seat and made his way toward the main door along with Zane, thier footsteps deliberate, steady. The knocking continued, a constant drumbeat in the background.

As he reached the door, he paused. His fingers brushed the cold metal handle, and for a moment, he hesitated. He had to be sure. The stakes were too high to make a rash move, especially when trust was still in short supply. Without a word, he turned the handle and opened the door just enough to reveal the two figures standing outside.

Connor and Elias stood in the threshold, their faces half-lit by the dim light from the setting sun. They looked weary, their clothes torn and dirty, but there was something else about them—a quiet sense of resolve. Connor was the first to speak, his voice calm, though it carried an edge of weariness.

"We weren't sure if you'd let us in, but we made it here," he said, his eyes flickering briefly to the others standing behind Atlas. "We weren't followed. At least, not by anyone we can see."

Atlas studied them for a long moment. Connor had the build of a man who had been through some tough times—muscular, weathered, but with a certain kindness in his eyes that Atlas couldn't quite place. Elias, on the other hand, was taller, lankier, with sharp features that seemed perpetually tense. He didn't say anything, just waited for Connor to speak for him.

Zane, who had been watching the exchange closely, leaned in toward Atlas, his voice a low murmur. "I don't know, man. They look okay, but—"

"I know," Atlas replied, his tone quiet but firm. He still wasn't convinced.

"Alex and Taylor trust them," Zane added, almost pleading. "We should at least hear them out."

Atlas turned back toward Connor and Elias, his eyes narrowing. "You said you were gathering supplies. Why didn't you come with them to the tower? Why the delay?"

Connor's gaze flickered toward Elias, as if silently communicating something. After a moment, he answered, his voice steady. "We were trying to avoid drawing attention. The streets have become a hellhole. It's too dangerous to travel together in large groups. We made it out, but not without some close calls."

Elias finally spoke, his voice cold but not unfriendly. "We knew it would be better if we came separately. The fewer people we move with, the less likely we are to attract unwanted attention."

Atlas weighed their words, scanning their faces for any hint of deceit. Finally, he nodded, stepping back to allow them entry. "We'll talk inside."

Once inside, the door closed behind them with a quiet thud, and the tension in the room seemed to ease slightly, though not entirely. The group settled into a loose circle, with Connor and Elias sitting on one side, and the rest of the group on the other.

Connor and Elias began to share their stories. Connor, the firefighter, spoke about how he had survived the early days of the outbreak, helping people escape danger and trying to keep his community safe. Elias, the scientist, talked about how the outbreak had unfolded in ways no one had anticipated. His theories were unsettling, describing how the virus had mutated, causing the infected to become not just mindless predators but more organized, even capable of some rudimentary tactics.

As the night wore on, the conversation took a darker turn. They spoke of areas where the infection seemed to have spread faster, where survivors were in short supply, and where new dangers were emerging—dangers that were not just the zombies, but other survivors driven by desperation.

"What do you mean, other survivors?" Finn asked, his voice sharp. "What kind of people are we talking about?"

Elias looked uneasy, shifting in his seat. "Not all survivors are good people. Some have turned... cold. Ruthless. I've seen people who would rather kill to get what they need than help others. Trust me, the infected aren't the only threat out there."

Connor nodded in agreement. "The world's a dangerous place, more than you realize."

The group listened intently, each one processing the weight of the information. A heavy silence followed, as if everyone in the room was trying to comprehend the full scope of what they were hearing. The zombies were bad enough, but now there were human threats as well. The world was descending into something far worse than anyone had imagined.

But just as the conversation seemed to settle, a sudden shift in the atmosphere broke the quiet. The monitor in the corner flickered on, and Zane's eyes went wide as he looked at the screen. His fingers hovered over the control panel, adjusting the camera angles.

"Something's wrong," Zane said, his voice laced with alarm.

The camera feed showed something that made everyone's blood run cold. The ground outside the tower was crawling with zombies, their numbers seemingly endless. They moved in a disjointed wave, shambling toward the tower in a way that felt far too coordinated. The feed showed the approaching threat clearly, and for a moment, no one spoke. "This is what we've been preparing for," Atlas said quietly, his voice filled with quiet determination. "It's time to act."

The group sprang into action, their previous concerns momentarily forgotten as they focused on the immediate danger outside. As the night grew darker, they could hear the sound of the zombies outside, their guttural growls seeping through the walls. But it wasn't just the zombies they were worried about now—it was everything they had been preparing for. The world outside was no longer just a wasteland of the infected; it was a battleground.

And it was getting closer.

CHAPTER XXIV

Shadows of the Monster

The sun had barely risen the next morning when the tension from the previous night's events lingered like a thick fog in the air. The knock on the door, the arrival of Connor and Elias—it had all left a heaviness that seemed impossible to shake. Atlas, Connor, and Elias had spent most of the night strategizing, discussing the plan. The zombies that had appeared at the main door the night before had only been the beginning. From the camera feed, they'd seen more zombies gathered outside, drawn by the noise of the knocking, the movements, the scent of life.

Now, the time had come to deal with them.

Atlas stood at the front of the group, his posture rigid. His face was set, his jaw clenched as he stared out of the science tower's window. The morning light illuminated the scene below, but it didn't bring any warmth to his heart. Outside, the zombies roamed aimlessly, some stumbling, others more alert, all of them drawn toward the tower by the scent of the living.

"We take them out now," Atlas said, his voice firm, cold. He didn't look at anyone when he spoke—his words weren't for reassurance, they were a command. There was no softness in his tone, only a ruthless determination that chilled the air around him.

Connor and Elias exchanged a quick glance, but neither said a word. They had been in situations like this before—kill or be killed. The new group of survivors had yet to fully witness what Atlas was capable of.

The others watched from the windows, their eyes glued to the scene below. None of them moved. The silence was suffocating, but no one dared speak. They all knew what was about to happen.

Connor adjusted his gear, checking the weapons at his side. He was quick and efficient, his eyes focused on the task ahead. Elias, more laid-back, but just as lethal, shrugged his shoulders and prepared to follow Atlas. They had already planned their approach: clear the area, kill them all, and make sure the surrounding area was safe for the group. It would take all three of them to ensure the zombies didn't swarm the tower.

Atlas didn't waste any time. He motioned for the others to follow, but they stayed behind, watching from the safety of The Skylight. Atlas, Connor, and Elias descended the stairs to the tower's main floor, their footsteps heavy and deliberate. The sound of their boots on the concrete echoed through the empty halls.

When they reached the main entrance, the door was still slightly ajar, the faint smell of the zombies lingering in the air. They peered outside. The zombies were clustered near the base of the tower, their numbers growing with each passing minute. They had to be taken out before they got any closer.

"Ready?" Atlas asked, his voice a whisper as he checked the weapons on his belt. The others nodded.

Without another word, they stepped outside, emerging into the open space just outside the tower. The morning light filtered through the haze, casting long shadows across the ground. The zombies, oblivious to the approaching danger, continued to shuffle aimlessly, their vacant eyes fixed on nothing.

Atlas moved first. His steps were measured, purposeful, his expression cold and calculating. The first zombie came into view—a stumbling, groaning figure, its decaying body moving sluggishly. Atlas didn't hesitate. With a quick motion, he drew his knife and lunged forward. The blade found its target in the zombie's skull with a sickening crack, and it fell to the ground without a sound.

Connor and Elias followed suit, each dispatching their own targets with precision. They worked as a team, moving swiftly, silently, their movements fluid and practiced. Every swing, every stab, was an execution. The zombies fell one by one, their bodies piling up in the dirt.

The rest of the group watched from the window, their gazes fixed on Atlas. There was something unsettling in the way he moved, in the way he seemed to relish each kill. His face was impassive, his body stiff, almost mechanical as he cleared the zombies in rapid succession.

Jax shifted uncomfortably, glancing over at Zane. "Is it just me, or does Atlas seem... different?" His voice was low, as though speaking louder might disturb the unsettling stillness of the moment.

Zane didn't respond right away, his eyes locked on Atlas. The words seemed to be stuck in his throat. He didn't know what to make of it. It was like watching a soldier who had forgotten any semblance of humanity. Atlas moved with a detached efficiency that was chilling, his eyes distant, his hands steady as he stabbed and slashed. It wasn't just that he was killing—it was the way he did it, as though it didn't matter who or what he was fighting anymore.

Finn's voice broke through the silence, his usual calm replaced by a hint of unease. "I didn't expect... this. He's not holding back."

"None of us can afford to hold back," Zane replied quietly, though his voice lacked the usual conviction. He was still watching Atlas, unable to shake the sense that something had shifted in the man who had been their leader. "But... this... this is different."

Jess stood beside them, her arms crossed as she watched. She felt a strange pang in her chest. Atlas had always been steady, reliable. But now, in this moment, she saw something else. A coldness. A ruthlessness she hadn't known him for. It was unsettling, yet she understood. The world had changed them all.

"Don't get too attached to the idea of mercy," Elias called out from below. He was wiping blood from his hands, his face expressionless. "In this world, mercy doesn't do you any good."

Atlas didn't acknowledge the comment. He was already moving on to the next group of zombies, methodically clearing the area, one kill after another. The sound of flesh tearing, the sickening crack of bones breaking—these were the sounds that filled the air now. The zombies didn't stand a chance.

The group watched, transfixed, as Atlas continued his ruthless onslaught. It was a brutal display, one that left them all speechless. It was almost as though he was fighting a war—fighting not just for survival but for something deeper. Something darker.

When the last of the zombies finally fell, the group remained silent. Atlas stood in the middle of the battlefield, breathing heavily, his chest rising and falling with each breath. His hands were covered in blood, his clothes stained, but his expression remained as unreadable as ever.

He turned and looked back at the tower, his eyes meeting those of the others watching from above. There was no pride in his gaze, no satisfaction. Only coldness.

"We're safe for now," Atlas said, his voice flat. "But we can't let our guard down."

As the group descended from above to join him, the tension in the air was palpable. There was an unspoken realization among them. Atlas had done what needed to be done, but in the process, something about him had changed. He was no longer just the leader. He had become something else. Something darker.

And in the silence that followed, someone finally spoke the words that had been on all their minds.

"He's a monster," Jax muttered, almost under his breath.

But as he said it, there was no fear in his voice. There was a strange kind of reverence. The kind of respect one might give to a force of nature. A force that was necessary for survival.

And in that moment, the group understood. They needed him. They needed the monster Atlas had become.

CHAPTER XXV

Working Shadows

The group sat in stunned silence, their eyes occasionally darting to Atlas, who remained unusually quiet, lost in his thoughts. The brutal scene from the previous day still hung over them like a dense fog, the sharp edges of it cutting through the calm of the science tower. Even as the day passed and the usual routines of survival resumed, there was an underlying unease. The transformation Atlas had undergone in the heat of the moment was unsettling. To some, he had become a protector. To others, a monster.

It was in the midst of this uneasy silence that Conner and Elias stepped forward, the two new survivors breaking the stillness with an unexpected revelation.

"There's something we should show you," Conner said, his voice low but urgent. "A radio in the tower. It's the most powerful one in the city."

Atlas looked up, his brow furrowing in confusion. "A radio? We've been here for weeks, and how come you've known this?"

Elias gave a small, knowing grin. "We had to be sure," he replied cryptically. "And frankly, that's why we have come to this tower in the first place."

Zane stood up, his interest piqued. "A radio? The most powerful in the city? How come we haven't heard anything from it?"

Conner stepped closer to the group. "It was always there. You just never checked. It's connected to a network of communication that can still reach some of the surviving settlements. The problem is, it hasn't been functional. Until now."

Chase leaned forward, raising an eyebrow. "You're telling us we could've been calling for help this whole time? For days, and we didn't even know?"

"We weren't sure either," Elias added, shaking his head. "But now we do. And fixing it is a priority. It could give us the answers we need—locations of survivors, food drops, anything that might help us get out of this mess."

Atlas stood, his mind racing. "We can't ignore this," he muttered, more to himself than anyone else. "We need to fix it, and fast."

Suddenly, Elias smirked, as if he had something up his sleeve. "And, by the way," he said, locking eyes with Atlas, "you guys didn't exactly strike me as the sharpest tools in the shed. The author didn't make you guys smart, did he? You all just stumble into everything."

The room fell deathly silent. Everyone's eyes turned toward Elias, but it was Atlas who reacted first, his gaze narrowing, lips pressing into a tight line. "What did you just say?"

Elias waved a hand dismissively. "Oh, nothing. Just a joke. Don't mind me."

But Atlas couldn't shake the feeling that something was off. How did Elias know about the radio? He hadn't even hinted at it before. It didn't sit right with him. He exchanged a glance with Zane, who caught his suspicion, and the two of them silently agreed—something wasn't adding up.

"Fixing the radio is a good idea," Zane said, his voice calm but with an edge. "I'll help you with that."

"Great!," Elias added. "I know my way around communication systems. Let's see if we can get this working."

Meanwhile, Chase stood in the background, watching the interaction between Elias and Atlas with narrowed eyes. He had a feeling things were about to get a lot more complicated than anyone realized.

"Atlas," Jax said suddenly, breaking the tension, "why don't you and I head to the terrace again? The helicopter isn't going to learn how to fly itself, right?"

Atlas nodded, grateful for the distraction. "Right. Let's go."

As they headed out toward the terrace, Finn stood up, a determined look on his face. "I've got a plan for the car," he said to Conner, who was standing nearby. "We need to get the Explorer ready for what's coming. We can't rely on just walking everywhere. I'll need your help."

Conner gave a curt nod. "Let's get to it. We'll need to reinforce the wheels, upgrade the armor, and make sure it's equipped to handle anything. "

The group had split into their tasks, but the undercurrent of tension remained. Atlas couldn't shake the thought of Elias' words. What did he mean? How did they know things they shouldn't?

As Atlas and Jax made their way up to the terrace, the night air was cool and crisp, the faint hum of the city in the distance. It had been a long few days, but the helicopter had become a symbol of hope for Atlas. If they could learn how to fly it, it might be their ticket to survival, a way to get out of the chaos that had consumed the world.

Jax clapped him on the back as they reached the terrace. "Let's get this bird in the air, man."

Atlas grinned, his earlier unease momentarily forgotten. "Let's do this."

Meanwhile, inside the tower, the rest of the group gathered around the large radio. Elias and Zane worked together, fiddling with wires and dials, while Chase watched, his arms crossed.

Back on the terrace, Atlas and Jax were absorbed in their work, reading the helicopter's manuals and checking the controls. Atlas couldn't help but feel a sense of urgency—if they were going to get out of this, they needed to be ready for anything. And they couldn't afford to waste time.

As night fell over the city, the group worked tirelessly. The clock was ticking, and the world outside was growing darker by the hour.

CHAPTER XXVI

Shadows of Despair

A month had passed since the group first began their frantic efforts to survive. Each day had felt like a blur, consumed with constant work and the grinding reality of their situation. But amidst the chaos and the constant pressure, there were moments of fleeting relief.

The sound of tools clanging, engines roaring, and wires being fixed had become a constant hum in the background of their lives, but it wasn't all doom and gloom. In fact, there were moments of quiet joy, moments where the weight of the world seemed to lift, if only for a little while.

Finn and Jess had become inseparable over the past month. They'd spent more time working on the car together, brainstorming ways to improve the Explorer and turn it into the ultimate apocalypse vehicle. Finn would make silly jokes to keep the mood light, and Jess would roll her eyes, a smile tugging at the corner of her lips.

"Hey, Jess, think we could add a machine gun to the roof?" Finn asked, his grin wide as he tightened a bolt on the front bumper.

Jess shot him a playful look. "You do realize that we'll probably need to save those bullets for zombies, right?"

"I'm just saying," Finn shrugged, "if we're gonna go down, might as well look badass doing it."

Jess chuckled, shaking her head. "You're unbelievable, you know that?"

Finn leaned in closer, his voice lowering. "And you love it."

Before Jess could respond, she playfully nudged him, knocking his shoulder with hers. "Stop trying to charm me, Finn," she teased. "It's not gonna work."

Finn's grin softened, and for a moment, there was only the sound of their quiet laughter, the weight of the world fading away.

Meanwhile, Alex and Taylor had found their own moments of connection as well. They'd taken to sitting together during the quieter evenings, often talking about things that no longer seemed to matter—music they liked before everything fell apart, memories of family dinners, or places they once dreamt of visiting.

One night, as the sun set behind the science tower, Alex and Taylor sat side by side on the rooftop, gazing out over the desolate landscape. The distant hum of the generator below was the only noise breaking the silence.

"I miss the ocean," Taylor said softly, her voice barely above a whisper. "I used to spend hours by the shore, just listening to the waves."

Alex turned to her, a faint smile on his lips. "I used to hate the ocean. Too salty, too... unpredictable. But now, I think I'd give anything to hear those waves again."

Taylor laughed, a soft, melancholic sound. "Funny how things change, right?"

Alex nodded, but there was a sadness in his eyes. "Yeah, it's like we're just drifting now, waiting for something to change. But who knows? Maybe it's better if we don't get our hopes up."

Taylor leaned her head on his shoulder, and the simple gesture, the quiet comfort of being with someone in the midst of all this madness, was enough to make the world feel a little more bearable. "We'll get through this, Alex," she whispered. "We have to."

On the other side of the tower, the mood was much lighter as the group took a break from their relentless work. Zane, Chase, and Elias had become engrossed in their mission to fix the radio. Every day, they chipped away at it, trying to find the missing piece of the puzzle. But despite their tireless efforts, the radio had yet to send a single coherent message.

Elias wiped his brow dramatically, as if it were the end of a long day, and said, "Well, at least the radio's now making more noise than my brain."

Zane shot him an annoyed look, clearly not amused. "Thanks, Elias. That's really helpful."

Chase, never one to pass up a good opportunity, grinned. "Maybe it's your charm, Elias. You know, with all the static, the radio might just be trying to escape from you."

Elias gasped in mock offense. "Oh, I see how it is. I offer my undivided comedic genius, and you all choose to tear me down. Fine, then. I'll just leave you to your precious static!"

Zane rolled his eyes, but there was a small smile tugging at the corner of his mouth. "Would you two just focus? I swear, it's like herding cats trying to get any real work done with you two."

For a moment, it seemed like their constant bickering was the only thing that kept them sane. It was a rare sight—Chase and Elias bickering like friends, and Zane trying his best to keep them in line. But despite their humorous exchanges, the frustration was starting to settle in.

After another long day of work, the trio gathered in front of the radio once more. The screen flickered, and the machine buzzed loudly. But instead of the crackling sound of voices or even a transmission, there was nothing but silence.

Chase wiped his hands on his pants, the weight of their fruitless efforts settling on his shoulders. "Maybe it's time we admit it," he said quietly, his voice laced with frustration. "Maybe the radio's just... dead."

Elias stepped back, shaking his head. "No, it can't be. We've put too much into this. We've come so far."

Zane's fingers hovered over the controls, his mind racing as he tried to recalibrate the frequencies once more. But with every attempt, the radio remained silent.

"We need something to hope for," Elias said, his tone unexpectedly serious. "If we don't have that, what's the point?"

The silence stretched between them, and Atlas, who had been watching from the doorway, couldn't help but overhear their words. He felt the weight of their despair in his chest, like a heavy stone lodged deep inside him. How much longer could they keep going like this? The radio wasn't just a machine; it was their connection to the outside world, the last thread that might lead them to safety. Without it, what was left?

"Maybe the radio's not the answer," Atlas said softly, his voice carrying through the room. He had been silent for most of the day, his mind focused on the heavy work at hand. But now, the weight of Elias' words seemed to settle deep within him.

The group looked at him, their faces a mix of confusion and desperation. Atlas paused, glancing over his shoulder to the others—Jax, Finn, and the rest of the crew—who had gathered in the shadows, their expressions unreadable.

"We can't keep depending on something that might never work," Atlas continued. "Maybe it's time we start thinking about other ways to survive."

It was a heavy statement, and the room fell silent once more, the hum of the generator the only sound breaking the tension.

But just as quickly as the quiet descended, the sound of Finn's voice broke the stillness. "So, what do we do now?" he asked, leaning against the doorframe with his arms crossed.

Atlas' gaze was unwavering as he met Finn's eyes. "We keep fighting. We fix the car, we figure out how to fly that helicopter, and we keep moving forward. We don't wait for something to happen. We will make it happen."

As the group nodded in agreement, Elias offered a wry smile. "Well, if we're going to make it happen, I'm going to need a lot more caffeine."

The others laughed, but it was a nervous, strained sound. Even in the face of despair, they knew they had no other choice but to keep moving. The road ahead was uncertain, and the shadows seemed to grow longer with each passing day. But for now, they had each other.

And that was enough.

CHAPTER XXVII

Emerging Shadows

It had been another long day of hard work, and the group had made significant progress. Atlas had finally started to get the hang of flying the helicopter, though it wasn't smooth sailing just yet. With each attempt, he felt a little more confident, but there was always that lingering fear in the back of his mind—what if they needed to take off quickly? What if something went wrong?

But for now, it was good enough. Jax had helped him out, offering advice with a level of patience that Atlas could hardly believe. Even so, flying wasn't quite the same as leading the group through danger on the ground. It was a different kind of responsibility.

Meanwhile, Finn and Conner had been busy putting the finishing touches on the Explorer. The car was almost ready, the new armor plating fitted onto the sides, and the engine purring louder and stronger than before. The tires had been reinforced, and they'd even managed to make modifications to the exhaust system. The Explorer was no longer just a car—it was a weapon on wheels.

"You know," Finn said, wiping his hands on his pants as he stood back to admire the car. "If I didn't know better, I'd say we've got ourselves a tank on wheels."

Conner gave a tired laugh, his face smeared with grease. "Tank? Maybe. But at least it'll get us through the worst of it. No more getting stuck on the road."

"Good thing," Finn muttered, glancing over at the horizon, "'cause we can't afford to slow down. Not now."

As the two of them continued to work, Jess found herself gravitating toward Finn, as she often did during these quiet moments. She had spent so much of the past few weeks caught up in the grind, the fear, and the uncertainty. But with Finn, there was an odd sense of calm—a sense that, for a few moments, things could be normal again.

"So, Ryder-boy," Jess said softly, her voice breaking the comfortable silence, "how do you think we're doing? I mean, with everything going on."

Finn didn't look up immediately but gave her a sideways glance, a small grin on his face. "I think we're making it through, Jess. We're all still here, aren't we? That counts for something."

"Yeah," Jess agreed, her voice quiet. "But it's hard sometimes, you know? I keep thinking about... about what's out there. What we could be walking into."

Finn stood, wiping his hands on a rag before he placed a reassuring hand on her shoulder. "You know, I've been thinking the same thing. We've got the tools, the skills. We just have to keep moving forward. You've got to trust that we'll get through this."

Jess smiled faintly, looking up at him. "You really think so?"

"I don't just think it," Finn replied, his voice steady and confident. "I know it."

His words felt like a promise, and for the first time in a long while, Jess allowed herself to believe it.

As the day drew to a close, the rest of the group gathered in the common area, ready for the first meal they'd shared together in a long time. There was a slight sense of normalcy that hung in the air—dinner didn't feel like just another routine to keep them going. It felt like a moment of unity, a time to take a breath and reconnect with each other.

Elias had finally stopped tinkering with the radio, taking a break from his work. He was tired, but the thought of completing the task was what kept him going. Every time they'd gotten close to fixing it, the radio would cut out again, or they'd run into some other obstacle. But tonight, he seemed ready to share something that had been weighing on his mind.

"You know," Elias said as he took a seat at the table, "when Conner and I went out a few days ago to gather supplies, we ran into something a little different."

The table grew quieter, and everyone shifted their focus toward him.

"What do you mean?" Chase asked, his curiosity piqued.

Elias took a deep breath, leaning forward slightly. "We came across a group of zombies, sure. But then, we saw one. Off in the distance. This one... it was bigger. More dangerous looking. It had this energy to it, like it wasn't just a regular zombie. It felt... intentional. It knew what it was doing."

The group exchanged uneasy glances. Atlas could feel a tightness in his chest, as if something about this story didn't sit right with him. His mind immediately went to the worst possible scenario.

"Sounds like a boss zombie," Jax muttered. "Great, just what we need."

But Atlas's thoughts were somewhere else entirely. His mind raced with possibilities. No. It can't be him. Please let it not be him.

"I don't know what it was," Elias continued, "but it was different. Almost like it was waiting for something."

That sent a chill through the room. Everyone seemed to sense the same unease. No one spoke for a few moments, as the weight of Elias's words hung heavy in the air.

"Maybe it's a new breed," Zane finally said, trying to break the tension. "Maybe these things are evolving."

Atlas clenched his fists under the table. Evolving. Or orchestrating. He couldn't push the thought from his mind.

"Let's just pray we don't have to find out," Finn said quietly, looking over at Atlas. "Whatever it is, we can handle it. Just like we've handled everything else."

The room was silent for a moment before Atlas nodded, though his mind remained elsewhere, lost in the implications of what Elias had said.

The rest of the evening passed in quiet conversation. Conner and Jess laughed softly in the corner, their voices light and easy. Alex and Taylor shared a moment of peace, and the rest of the group found small ways to relax, to find solace in each other's company.

Dinner was finished, the dishes cleared, and the sound of the wind outside seemed to deepen the stillness of the room. Everyone had that feeling again—the weight of time hanging over them, the unspoken knowledge that things were bound to change soon.

It was then, just as the last of the evening's chatter began to die down, that the radio crackled to life. At first, it was a burst of static, just like the dozens of failed attempts they had already encountered. But this time, something was different. There was a rhythm to it, a pulse behind the noise.

Then, just as the group had started to dismiss it as another false alarm, the static shifted. A voice broke through.

"Hello?"

The voice was clearer now. It sounded familiar, but it was hard to place.

And that was when the silence truly settled in—no one knew who was on the other side, or what they wanted.

But Atlas knew one thing for sure: this was the moment they had been waiting for. And everything was about to change.

CHAPTER XXVIII

Shadows of Hope

The air was thick with anticipation as the voice crackled once again through the static on the radio. The group's collective breath seemed to catch in their throats. Atlas leaned forward, his heart pounding in his chest as the voice continued, now clearer and more distinct.

"Hello, is anyone there?"

It wasn't a voice they recognized, but there was something oddly familiar about the cadence. A part of Atlas had feared it would be a trap, but he couldn't ignore the fact that the voice carried a certain authority, a confidence that made his stomach flutter with both hope and apprehension.

"Who is this?" Atlas spoke first, his voice steady despite the turmoil roiling inside him.

The voice on the other end took a breath, a slight pause before he replied, "This is Knox Mercer. I've been trying to reach you for a while."

The name hit Atlas like a punch to the gut. Knox Mercer—the friend he had trusted most. Despite everything that had happened, the sound of his voice brought a mix of memories, some sweet and some bitter. But Knox had always been a natural leader, and the fact that he was reaching out now brought a glimmer of hope to Atlas's heart.

"Knox?" Atlas echoed, trying to mask the surprise in his voice. He hadn't expected to hear from him again. "We've been looking for a way to communicate. How did you get this radio working?"

"I've got my ways," Knox replied cryptically, as if nothing had changed between them. "Listen, I'm not here to waste your time. I've got a place, a survival camp, about two days' drive from your location. It's a safe zone—people, food, water, weapons. I've got a community here, people trying to survive, just like you. I'm offering you a chance to join us."

The group exchanged looks, the words settling into their minds. They had known Knox for years before the outbreak. He was a survivor, a leader in his own right, and someone they had trusted. The radio crackled again.

"We'll need time to prepare," Atlas said after a long silence, his voice firm. "Five days, then. We'll make sure we're ready to move."

"Sounds good," Knox replied. "I'll be waiting. You know where to find me."

With that, the radio crackled one last time and went silent. The air in the room felt thick, the weight of the decision settling over the group. Knox had always been the one with the plan, the one who could turn nothing into something. They didn't know exactly what to expect, but if anyone could survive in this world, it was Knox.

"We're doing this?" Finn asked, his voice quiet.

"We don't have much choice," Jax replied, his voice steady, but there was a glimmer of uncertainty in his eyes. "Knox was always the leader. We need to believe in that. We need this."

Jess nodded. "We've been doing this on our own for so long. Maybe it's time to take a chance."

"I agree," Conner chimed in, glancing over at Finn, who gave him a nod of agreement. "Knox's place might be just what we need. If we don't go now, we could lose the chance."

"We're ready," Atlas said, his tone resolute. "Five days. We get everything prepared. We don't leave until we're ready."

The decision was made, and there was no turning back. The group spent the next few days focused on preparing for the journey. Atlas worked tirelessly with Jax to ensure the helicopter was in flying condition, while Finn, Conner, and Jess worked on the Explorer, making sure it was armored and reinforced for the treacherous road ahead. The air was heavy with determination as the group raced against the clock to get everything in order.

At the same time, Max spent hours making sure their weapons were properly loaded, knowing that the road to Knox's camp would be a dangerous one. The sounds of tools, engines, and weapons filled the air as the group worked in unison, each person focused on their task. It was clear that they were a team—survivors who had come together against all odds.

During this time, the relationships within the group began to flourish. Jess and Finn spent moments alone, their quiet conversations filled with understanding and a growing sense of closeness. Their shared moments, though brief, were enough to remind them both of the world they had once known—a world where survival wasn't the only thing on their minds.

Later, as the day drew to a close, the group gathered around the small campfire they had set up on the terrace of the tower, the warm glow of the flames offering a comforting contrast to the bleak world they faced. The conversation was light, the atmosphere more relaxed than it had been in days. Atlas leaned back, listening to the sound of the fire crackling, and allowed himself to take a breath.

"We'll be okay," Finn said, his voice steady as he gazed into the fire. "We've got each other. We've been through worse."

"That's true," Max agreed. "We've survived so far because we stick together."

As the conversation continued, Atlas found himself glancing over at the helicopter, the machine that would carry them away from the tower and into the unknown. He wasn't sure what awaited them at Knox's camp, but he knew they couldn't stay in the tower forever. They had to move forward, even if it meant facing the unknown.

After a few days, they will be on their way to Survivor's Haven—Knox's camp. And with it, they hoped, a future.

CHAPTER XXIX

The Twist in The Shadows

The dawn broke over the science tower, casting its familiar golden light across the campus grounds as the group made their final preparations. The day had finally come. Each of them could feel the mixture of excitement and nervousness in the air—a heavy anticipation that made their actions feel both fast and slow, as if they were on the edge of something monumental.

Atlas moved through the skylight, gathering the last of their things, a quiet sort of determination settling into him. This place had been their home, their fortress, their last stand for so long, and saying goodbye felt strange, almost surreal. It was as though they were shedding an old life, leaving behind their first chapter of survival. But they had Knox's camp to look forward to—a promised refuge, where they could start fresh. For now, Atlas pushed any unease to the back of his mind and focused on the task at hand.

The Explorer was loaded with supplies—food, water, weapons, and everything else they'd need for the journey. Atlas, Jax, Conner, and Elias would be taking the helicopter, with Atlas at the controls, as he had managed to gain enough skill to fly it with some ease. Finn, Jess, Chase, Zane, Max, Alex, and Taylor would take the Explorer, with Finn handling the driving. As Atlas's group moved to the terrace, where the helicopter awaited, the others headed to the parking lot below, casting one last look at the tower they had called home.

"Ready, Atlas?" Jax asked, a grin on his face as he adjusted his gun and turned his gaze to the sunrise over the skyline. "One last flight from the terrace?"

Atlas nodded, though he was finding it harder than expected to leave The Skylight. It had become their home in every way—their place of safety, their lookout. He took a deep breath, his gaze lingering on the familiar hallways as if imprinting the memory into his mind. The silence was a reminder of both the solace and the chaos that this place had held.

As they reached the rooftop, Atlas noticed that Conner and Elias had been uncharacteristically quiet. They had moved ahead, unbarring the entrance to the terrace and making space for Atlas and Jax to follow. The helicopter blades began to whir, and Atlas focused on adjusting the controls, settling into the pilot's seat with Jax beside him, his attention entirely on the mission ahead.

But as Atlas leaned forward to adjust the switches, he sensed something shift—a tension in the air that felt wrong. Suddenly, from the corner of his eye, he saw the glint of a gun aimed directly at him.

"Atlas!" Jax's warning came just in time as Atlas ducked, narrowly avoiding the bullet that whizzed past him, hitting the metal frame of the helicopter with a sharp, resounding clang.

Atlas's mind raced as he took in the sight before him. Conner and Elias stood at the edge of the terrace, their expressions cold, detached, their guns aimed directly at him and Jax. The confusion and betrayal stung, the realization hitting him like a physical blow.

"Conner, Elias...what the hell are you doing?" Atlas demanded, his voice raw with anger and disbelief.

Conner smirked, his demeanor shifting from quiet ally to something darker, more ruthless. He glanced at Elias, who gave him a nod, their silent agreement chilling in its clarity. They had planned this.

"We've had enough of following your lead, Atlas," Conner said, his tone casual, as if they were discussing nothing more serious than a game. "We're done being pawns in your little survival game. We're taking control now, and that means getting rid of the dead weight."

Atlas's heart pounded as he reached for his weapon, but Conner fired another shot, grazing his arm. Jax retaliated, shooting back and forcing Conner and Elias to take cover behind the rooftop's ventilation units. The air was thick with tension, the whirr of the helicopter blades and the echo of gunfire creating a cacophony against the early morning silence.

"What is this really about, Conner?" Atlas demanded, his voice cold as he moved closer to Jax, taking cover behind the helicopter. "Is this some power play?"

Elias laughed, a mocking sound that sent a shiver down Atlas's spine. "Power play? Maybe. Or maybe we're just tired of playing hero when we don't need to. Survival's a game, Atlas, and only the strongest survive."

Atlas and Jax exchanged a quick glance, each understanding the weight of the situation. Their supposed friends, people they had trusted with their lives, had betrayed them in the most brutal way possible. And it was clear that Conner and Elias weren't interested in reasoning—they had already decided on their course of action.

As Jax covered him, Atlas fired a shot, catching Elias off-guard and grazing his leg. Elias cursed, stumbling back, but his expression turned from shock to a menacing grin. "Oh, this just got interesting."

Meanwhile, Atlas realized that Conner and Elias had already anticipated every escape route. He could see, in the distance, the telltale movements of zombies flooding into the lower levels of the building. They had unbarred the main entrances and let the undead swarm in—a calculated move that left Atlas and Jax trapped on the terrace with limited options for escape.

"What the hell did you do?" Jax shouted, his voice filled with fury as he fired another shot, forcing Conner to duck behind a concrete barrier.

"We opened the doors," Conner replied, almost gleeful. "Brought in a welcoming committee, just for you."

Atlas's mind raced, analyzing every possible move. The rooftop had limited cover, and with the building filling with zombies, their options were rapidly shrinking. Every second spent here was a second closer to being overrun, and Conner and Elias knew it. They had set this trap with a calculated ruthlessness that Atlas hadn't expected.

Atlas and Jax moved to the opposite side of the terrace, keeping low, their backs against the helicopter as they scanned the area for any opening. But Conner and Elias seemed to have anticipated every move. The zombies were already surging through the stairwells, drawn by the noise of the helicopter, the gunshots, the scent of life.

Atlas clenched his jaw, his gaze moving to Jax, whose eyes were filled with anger, but also a shared understanding. They didn't have time to dwell on betrayal—they needed to focus on survival. Atlas signaled to Jax to stay low, readying himself to sprint toward the side of the terrace, hoping to find a clear vantage point.

Before they could make their move, Elias's voice rang out, sharp and taunting. "You two were always so predictable. Playing hero, trying to save everyone. But look where that's gotten you."

"You're wrong," Atlas replied, his voice low and steady. "You don't survive by abandoning the people who trust you."

Elias sneered, his expression darkening. "Maybe not in your story. But this isn't your story anymore, Atlas. It's ours."

Atlas's pulse quickened as he caught sight of the zombies beginning to spill out onto the rooftop, their ravenous eyes locked onto the living targets in their midst. The situation was spiraling out of control faster than he could strategize, and he knew they had to act now or face a grim fate at the hands of both the undead and their former allies.

"Time to wrap this up," Conner said, his voice laced with satisfaction as he aimed his weapon at Atlas and Jax. "Goodbye, boys. It's been fun."

In a last-ditch move, Atlas grabbed a flare from his bag and tossed it toward the horde of zombies now crowding onto the terrace. The bright, searing light distracted the undead, their attention shifting momentarily away from him and Jax. In that split second, he and Jax dove for cover, using the brief diversion to position themselves closer to the helicopter's controls.

Elias cursed, realizing the shift in the fight. "You think a little light show is going to save you?" he taunted, but his voice betrayed a flicker of frustration.

Atlas used the moment to his advantage, turning back to face Conner and Elias with a cold, unyielding expression. "You might think you've won, but we're not finished yet."

Elias let out a dark chuckle, stepping forward, the glint of madness in his eyes. "Isn't it exciting, Atlas? The thrill of it all—the fight, the chaos, the chance to show who we really are."

His words hung in the air like a twisted anthem, a perverse celebration of the destruction and betrayal they had unleashed. Atlas felt the weight of those words settle over him, the chilling realization that this was only the beginning of a larger nightmare.

And as the zombies closed in around them, the terrace bathed in the eerie glow of the flare, he understood with a terrifying clarity that trust was a fragile thing—and in this new world, even the closest of friends could turn into enemies.

CHAPTER XXX

Broken Shadows

Atlas felt a chill run through him as he turned to face the scene ahead. Zombies crowded the terrace, drawn by the commotion and the lure of living flesh, their eyes wild and ravenous. Conner and Elias stood among them, their expressions twisted with dark satisfaction. Atlas knew he didn't have the luxury of feeling betrayed any longer—right now, his only priority was survival. The betrayal and anger would have to wait.

Beside him, Jax was ready, his jaw clenched and his hands steady on his weapon. They shared a quick glance, a silent agreement passing between them. They would fight their way through. There was no room for hesitation, not with the wave of undead and two armed traitors on the rooftop with them. They'd fought together through too much to be brought down here by people who had once been their friends.

Atlas steadied himself, gripping his weapon and diving into action. The next few minutes were a blur of motion, gunfire, and blood. He and Jax moved in perfect sync, taking down zombies with ruthless efficiency. Shots rang out in the early morning air as Atlas fired round after round, each bullet finding its mark with brutal precision. The horde was thick, but they had no choice but to clear a path through it.

Conner and Elias fought back as well, though their aim was anything but helping. Atlas noticed Conner's eyes trained on him as he tried to position himself behind a group of zombies, aiming for a clear shot. Conner's smirk was gone, replaced by an intense, almost feral look—one of a man who had chosen his path and was willing to face the consequences.

"You're still trying to survive?" Conner taunted, his voice carrying over the noise of the battle. "Give it up, Atlas! This was never going to end well for you!"

Atlas ignored him, focusing instead on the zombies lunging toward them. Every step was a struggle, every movement calculated to ensure he and Jax stayed alive. But even in the heat of the battle, the betrayal gnawed at him. Conner and Elias—people they'd trusted, fought beside—had turned on them, revealing themselves as opportunists willing to do anything for control.

Elias, meanwhile, moved through the chaos with a calculated calm, taking potshots at Atlas and Jax whenever he could. He was cunning, hiding behind the zombies to avoid a direct line of fire. Atlas could feel his fury building, but he kept his emotions in check, his mind focused on what he had to do. Rage wouldn't save them now; precision and a cold resolve would.

The helicopter provided some cover, but the zombies continued to pour onto the terrace, drawn by the noise and smell of life. Atlas fired in rapid succession, taking down a few zombies that had managed to break through their defensive line. Blood splattered across his arms as he moved, his senses heightened, his instincts on high alert.

Amid the chaos, Conner found his opportunity. He aimed his gun directly at Atlas, smirking as he pulled the trigger. But Atlas was faster. He shifted his weight, dodging the shot and retaliating with a quick, merciless shot of his own. The bullet struck Conner in the shoulder, sending him staggering back with a snarl of pain.

"You'll regret that," Conner spat, clutching his injured shoulder as he glared at Atlas. But there was fear in his eyes now, a realization that this might not go the way he'd planned.

"No, Conner," Atlas replied, his voice cold and unyielding. "You'll regret it."

Atlas took advantage of Conner's moment of weakness, closing the distance between them in a swift, brutal motion. Conner raised his weapon to defend himself, but Atlas was relentless, his fury honed into a deadly precision. He grabbed Conner, twisting his arm and forcing him to drop his gun. Conner's smug demeanor evaporated as Atlas slammed him against the railing, his gaze hard and unforgiving.

"This is for everything you've done," Atlas hissed, his voice low and fierce.

With a final, decisive motion, Atlas ended it. Conner's eyes widened in shock and fear, his last breath leaving him in a gasping, desperate exhale as he slumped against the railing, lifeless. Atlas felt no remorse, only a grim satisfaction. Conner had made his choice, and he had faced the consequences.

Meanwhile, Jax was locked in a vicious struggle with Elias. The two exchanged blows, their movements quick and brutal. Elias was fighting with a kind of reckless desperation, his smirk replaced by a wild, panicked look. He knew he was outmatched, but he fought with the stubbornness of someone who refused to accept his fate.

"Is this really how you wanted it to end, Elias?" Jax taunted, his voice sharp as he dodged a wild swing from his former friend. "Turning on us, becoming just another threat?"

Elias's response was a snarl as he lunged at Jax, but his movements were sloppy, fueled by anger rather than strategy. Jax took advantage of the opening, delivering a swift, brutal blow that sent Elias staggering back. Before he could recover, Jax followed up with a final, decisive strike, ending the fight with ruthless efficiency.

With the threat of Conner and Elias eliminated, Atlas and Jax turned their focus back to the remaining zombies. Together, they fought their way through the horde, each step bringing them closer to clearing the rooftop. The chaos was overwhelming, but they moved with the confidence of survivors who had faced down death before and refused to be defeated.

After what felt like an eternity, the last of the zombies fell, leaving the terrace littered with bodies. Atlas and Jax stood in the aftermath, their breaths heavy, their clothes splattered with blood. The betrayal still stung, but there was a grim sense of victory in having survived, in knowing that they had overcome yet another threat.

As the adrenaline began to wear off, the weight of what had just happened settled over them. Conner and Elias were gone, taken down by their own treachery. The thought should have been satisfying, but instead, it left a hollow ache, a reminder of how quickly trust could be shattered in this brutal new world.

Atlas glanced at Jax, who was wiping blood from his face, his expression grim. "You okay?"

Jax nodded, though his gaze was distant, his thoughts clearly lingering on the betrayal they had just witnessed. "Yeah. Just... didn't think it would come to this. Thought they'd have our backs."

"Me too," Atlas replied quietly. He looked out over the campus, his jaw clenched as he forced himself to focus on what needed to be done next. "But there's no time for regrets. We have to check on the others. They're depending on us."

Jax nodded, his resolve hardening. "Finn, Jess, Chase... they're all in the Explorer by now. But if Conner and Elias went this far, who knows what else they might have done?"

The thought sent a shiver down Atlas's spine. They had prepared for the journey with careful planning, loading the Explorer with everything they would need. But if Conner and Elias had set up traps or sabotaged their escape in any way, the others could be in serious danger.

Atlas and Jax descended the stairs, the metallic smell of blood and gunpowder heavy in the air, adrenaline still pulsing through their veins. Each step echoed, amplifying the chaotic sounds of battle below—the snarling growls of zombies, the sharp, unmistakable crack of gunfire, and the frantic shouts of their friends fighting for survival. The urgency of the situation pushed them to move faster, their earlier shock over Conner and Elias's betrayal momentarily set aside. They needed to reach the ground floor and get their people out, but doubt gnawed at Atlas. If Conner and Elias had been so willing to betray them, what other traps might they have left?

As they approached the last flight of stairs, Atlas could feel the tension tightening in his chest. This wasn't just a battle against the undead anymore; it was a test of their will to survive against the odds. Jax moved close behind him, his weapon ready, eyes narrowed and scanning for any movement. They'd lost enough today. They couldn't afford to lose anyone else.

On the ground floor, the scene was a chaotic blur. Max was positioned near the Explorer, his stance steady, firing at the horde of zombies encroaching from all directions.

The muzzle of his gun flared as he took down one zombie after another, his expression grim and determined. Finn was nearby, wielding an axe, swinging it with practiced intensity to clear a path toward the vehicle. Beside him, Chase was struggling with his pistol, visibly shaken but holding his ground, firing at anything that got too close. Jess was there too, wielding a crowbar, fierce and unrelenting.

"Over here!" Atlas called, catching their attention as he and Jax joined the fray. They didn't need to say anything—just the sight of them seemed to rekindle the group's resolve. The others rallied, fighting harder, working as a unit to thin the crowd of zombies.

Atlas took up a position near the Explorer, firing into the horde with calm precision. Every shot counted, and with each one, he felt a strange sense of satisfaction—an outlet for the betrayal, the anger, the fear that had been clawing at him all morning. He wasn't just fighting for survival; he was fighting to protect the people who had stayed loyal, those he knew he could still trust.

Beside him, Jax fought with a similar intensity, his usually light-hearted demeanor replaced by a cold focus. Together, they took down zombies with ruthless efficiency, creating a temporary buffer between the group and the advancing horde.

In the midst of the chaos, Atlas caught sight of Alex and Taylor at the back of the group. They were moving strangely, almost... disoriented. His gut twisted, but he brushed the thought aside, focusing on the task at hand. They were survivors, after all—just like the rest of them. But something about their movements tugged at the back of his mind, an instinctual warning he couldn't ignore.

"Everyone, get to the Explorer!" Atlas shouted, signaling for the group to begin their retreat toward the vehicle. Max kept firing, creating a protective cover as the others hurried toward the car. The urgency of the moment spurred them on, each of them aware of just how close they were to escaping this nightmare.

But as they neared the vehicle, Atlas's gaze fell on Alex and Taylor again. This time, he saw it clearly—the vacant, glassy look in their eyes, the slackened expressions on their faces. Their movements were no longer controlled or purposeful; instead, they were slow, almost mechanical, as if driven by something other than human consciousness.

Atlas froze, his mind struggling to process what he was seeing. A sickening realization washed over him, one that hit him harder than any bullet or blow.

"Alex... Taylor..." he murmured, his voice barely a whisper.

They weren't alive anymore. They were zombies.

It was a horrifying moment of clarity, the ground seeming to shift beneath him as the full weight of the truth settled. The people they had fought alongside, the friends they had protected, had become part of the very horde they were trying to escape.

CHAPTER XXXI

A Shadowed Fate

The chaos was relentless. Zombies pushed toward them from all directions, snarling and snapping, filling the air with the sickening stench of decay. Every member of the group fought with all they had, striking and shooting, their minds focused only on survival. Atlas moved like a machine, his movements precise, controlled, and unyielding. In his mind, every blow was one more step toward keeping his remaining family safe.

But amid the fighting, Atlas's gaze fell on Alex and Taylor. The realization from moments ago—that they were no longer human, no longer the people they had trusted—threatened to overwhelm him. Yet, he had no time to grieve. His mind sharpened, narrowing down to a single task: he had to do what was necessary.

"Zane!" he shouted, snapping Zane out of his own frantic attack. He jerked his head toward Alex and Taylor, and Zane's face twisted as he saw them. He'd known Alex and Taylor for months, and even though the situation was brutal, the thought of killing them now was unimaginable.

But there was no choice.

"I know," Zane said, his voice tight with pain and anger. He leveled his gun, his hands steady despite the emotion in his eyes. Atlas took a deep breath, focusing, pushing aside everything except the need to protect his group.

Together, he and Zane advanced toward their former friends. Taylor lunged forward, her once-friendly face now twisted into a grotesque mask, her eyes empty and devoid of any recognition. Atlas fired, his aim steady, feeling a pang of sorrow as her body fell. He had to force himself to look away from the lifeless shell on the ground, trying to hold himself together.

Zane raised his weapon toward Alex, his hand trembling only slightly before he squeezed the trigger. "I'm sorry, man," he murmured as the gunshot echoed in the room. Alex fell beside Taylor, a tragic end to the friends who had once been their allies, their confidants. The silence that followed seemed to pierce the air, but they couldn't stop. Not yet.

With Alex and Taylor taken down, the crowd of zombies began to thin out. Max and Finn held the line at the rear, making sure none slipped past them, while Chase and Jax kept the zombies from swarming them on either side. Every second felt like an eternity, but the flood of undead was finally lessening, their numbers shrinking.

As the attack eased, a feeling of cautious relief started to spread through the group. They were making progress. They could survive this. The remaining zombies fell one by one, and, as quiet settled around them, it seemed like they might finally have a moment to catch their breath.

Jess, ever practical, took a step toward the main gate to check if it was truly clear. "I think we're almost done here," she said, glancing back at the others with a tired but determined expression. "We should barricade this properly to keep them out."

"Good call," Finn agreed, panting as he wiped sweat from his brow. The group began moving toward Jess, feeling the strain of the battle but encouraged by the sight of their surroundings clearing out. Their victory felt close.

But just as Jess reached the gate, something massive lurched forward from the shadows outside. It wasn't like the other zombies they'd seen—it was larger, its limbs more defined and muscular, and its skin was a disturbing shade of grey, thickened like armor. Its eyes gleamed with a sick, twisted intelligence, a spark of malevolence that froze them all in place.

The creature moved fast, surging forward with horrifying strength. Before anyone could react, it was upon Jess. In an instant, its teeth sank into her neck, a brutal, vicious bite that sent a spray of blood across the ground.

Jess's scream cut through the air, raw and agonizing. The group stared in horror, paralyzed for a second by the brutal, unexpected attack. Atlas's heart dropped, dread settling over him as he realized who the creature was, even before he saw the familiar face twisted in monstrous rage.

"Cade..." Atlas whispered, barely able to believe it.

The creature—the Alpha zombie—was Cade. The friend who had once been a part of their family, who had been infected at the start of all this, had somehow transformed into something far more dangerous, far more terrifying than any of the other zombies they had faced. This was no mindless undead—it was a predator, and it had Jess in its grip.

"Jess!" Finn cried out, rushing forward, but the creature threw Jess aside like a rag doll, turning its gaze toward the group with a twisted, furious glare. The brutality in its movements, the predatory way it eyed them, made it clear that Cade was gone—this thing before them was no longer their friend.

The group fell into stunned silence, watching helplessly as Jess lay on the ground, blood pooling around her as her breathing grew shallow. Cade—the Alpha zombie—let out a deep, guttural growl, a challenge and a promise of the threat he posed.

CHAPTER XXXII

The Devil among The Shadows

The group stood frozen, their eyes locked onto the monstrous figure of Cade, or what Cade had become. A twisted, hulking creature, more powerful and brutal than anything they had ever encountered. His eyes, or the remains of them, burned with an unnatural hatred, a savage intelligence that sent chills through them all. No longer their friend, Cade had become something far worse: the embodiment of the nightmare that had engulfed their world.

Finn's gaze drifted over to Jess, who lay motionless on the ground, her chest barely rising with shallow, weakening breaths. Her neck was a horror of torn flesh, ravaged so severely by Cade's bite that it was clear she was slipping away. Her skin had paled, and her blood spilled like dark ink across the concrete. Finn dropped to his knees beside her, his hands trembling as he reached out to touch her cheek.

"Jess," he whispered, his voice breaking. She looked up at him with a faint, pain-stricken smile, her hand weakly reaching for his. She knew, as he did, that she was beyond saving. The brutal bite had sealed her fate. Yet, as her fingers brushed his, her gaze softened with a mix of apology and a deep, quiet acceptance.

"It's okay, Finn," she murmured, her voice faint. "You have to keep going...without me."

"No," Finn breathed, clutching her hand tightly, refusing to let her go. "I can't... I won't leave you here like this."

But Jess's eyes fluttered shut, her body going still as her breath faded. Finn felt the weight of his grief press down on him, an ache so raw it threatened to consume him. She had been the light, the warmth in this dark, unforgiving world. And now she was gone.

Atlas turned away, swallowing back the bitterness that threatened to break his resolve. He couldn't afford to mourn—not now. Cade's snarls filled the silence, the predator's eyes scanning the group, sizing them up. Atlas tightened his grip on his weapon, forcing himself to focus. He had lost too many already, and he would not lose the rest.

"Finn," Atlas called softly, pulling his friend from his grief, "we need you with us. Jess would want you to survive. To fight."

Finn nodded, though his face was a mask of pain, his eyes filled with rage. He rose, his fists clenched, and joined the others, his gaze now locked onto Cade. For a moment, none of them moved. Each one wrestled with the brutal truth: this monster, this creature, was once their friend. But the time for hesitation was gone.

As one, they advanced. The group encircled Cade, weapons raised, yet they hesitated, glancing at each other with flickers of doubt. Could they really kill him? Could they bring themselves to destroy what was left of their friend?

"Cade," Jax whispered, as though calling his name might somehow reach the part of him that was still human. But Cade only snarled, his lips pulling back to reveal jagged, bloodstained teeth.

Without warning, Cade lunged forward, his massive arm swinging in a deadly arc. The group scattered, barely dodging the blow. The ground shook with the force of his strike, leaving cracks in the concrete. Jax stumbled back, breathless as the reality of Cade's monstrous strength sank in.

"Damn it!" Zane muttered, gripping his weapon tighter. "We don't stand a chance against him."

"We don't have a choice," Atlas replied, gritting his teeth. "It's him or us."

They fought with everything they had, but Cade was relentless, absorbing blow after blow as if their weapons were mere annoyances. Bullets did little more than graze him, and even the strongest hits didn't slow him down. The group was growing exhausted, their strikes becoming desperate, and Cade seemed to feed off their fear, his brutal grin widening with each failed attack.

Atlas was thrown back against the wall, the impact knocking the breath from his lungs. Jax and Finn struggled to hold their ground, both narrowly avoiding Cade's deadly swipes. Chase and Zane exchanged fearful glances, realizing the brutal truth: Cade was not going down. And as much as they tried to fight, it was clear they were merely delaying the inevitable.

Finn glanced back at Jess, lying lifeless on the ground, and rage flooded his veins, giving him a brief surge of strength. "For Jess!" he roared, charging at Cade with all the fury he could muster. But Cade deflected him effortlessly, sending him sprawling across the floor.

One by one, the group fell back, defeated and exhausted. Cade let out a low, growling laugh, his eyes glinting with malicious satisfaction. This was his domain, and he was their executioner. They all felt it—that creeping, chilling despair. They couldn't win. They couldn't survive this.

Atlas's mind raced, desperate for any plan, any hope. But there was none. His strength was spent, his spirit wavering.

His friends lay beaten, Jess was gone, and Cade was still standing, a monstrous figure against the backdrop of ruin.

As they gathered themselves for what they believed would be their final stand, Atlas's gaze fell on a nearby corpse. Among the sprawled bodies of the undead lay one he hadn't noticed before—a figure in a torn, bloodied gi, with a familiar, worn face. It was Professor Han, their martial arts instructor from the university. In his cold, lifeless hand lay a katana, its blade reflecting the dim light. The weapon was still sharp, still deadly.

Atlas's eyes narrowed, and a flicker of determination reignited within him. He crawled over, reaching for the katana, his hand closing around the handle. He could feel its weight, solid and reassuring, a weapon meant for a true fight.

He rose, his gaze locking onto Cade. Atlas took a deep breath, his mind clearing, his purpose renewed. This was no longer a friend—this was a monster that needed to be put down, for the sake of his group, for Jess, for every moment of suffering they'd endured.

"I will finish you now," Atlas said, his voice cold and steady, his grip firm on the katana. Cade's grin faltered, as if he sensed the shift in Atlas's resolve. For the first time, the monster seemed to hesitate, but Atlas didn't give him a chance to react.

With a single, determined step, Atlas charged forward, the blade flashing through the air, ready to bring justice to the nightmare that Cade had become.

CHAPTER XXXIII

The Final Shadowfall

Atlas steadied himself, his grip tightening around the katana as he took a deep breath, drawing every ounce of focus he could muster. Cade loomed before him, a terrifying, twisted shadow of their former friend, his one remaining arm flexing as if taunting Atlas to strike. The intensity of Cade's glare was enough to chill anyone to the bone, but Atlas refused to waver. His mind was set, his heart hardened—he would finish this fight.

With a swift, powerful swing, Atlas brought the katana down, slicing through the air with deadly precision. The blade met Cade's arm in a sickening crack, severing it just below the shoulder. Cade let out a feral, guttural roar, a sound that seemed to echo through the ruins around them. His eyes blazed with unrestrained fury, the pain only fueling his rage.

Atlas barely had a moment to recover as Cade lunged forward, his body twisted in a monstrous dance of speed and power. With his remaining hand, Cade swung wildly, aiming to crush Atlas with sheer force. Atlas ducked and rolled, narrowly avoiding the blow, the katana steady in his hands as he prepared to strike again. But Cade was relentless, advancing with brutal ferocity, his movements unpredictable, his rage palpable.

"Atlas!" Jax's voice called out, and Atlas glanced to his side just in time to see his friend throwing him a spare machete. Catching it with his free hand, Atlas now wielded two blades, determined to match Cade's monstrous power with a fierceness of his own.

Cade was relentless, charging at Atlas with unbridled fury, his roars echoing as he swung his stump of an arm wildly, attempting to ram his way through Atlas's defenses. Atlas took advantage of his dual weapons, slashing at Cade's torso and legs whenever he could, trying to weaken his opponent's balance. But Cade hardly seemed to notice; each cut only seemed to make him angrier, his movements even more erratic and savage.

"Hold him back!" Zane shouted, and the rest of the group sprang into action. They surrounded Cade, their weapons drawn, trying to contain him. Chase and Max hacked at Cade's legs, while Jax and Finn lunged in, aiming for his back, doing anything to keep him off balance and to buy Atlas precious seconds to regain his footing.

Despite their best efforts, Cade seemed unstoppable. With a mighty swing, he threw Jax aside, sending him sprawling against the wall. Max barely dodged a wild kick that sent debris scattering across the floor. Cade's monstrous strength was undeniable, and every movement seemed to sap the group's energy and hope.

Finn swung his metal pipe at Cade's knee, and Cade stumbled for a moment, his balance faltering. Atlas seized the opportunity, lunging forward and slicing at Cade's torso, driving the blade deep. Blood sprayed across the floor, but Cade merely snarled, his remaining arm swinging with vicious speed. Atlas barely dodged, but the shockwave of the attack sent him stumbling.

"C'mon, Atlas!" Chase yelled, throwing himself at Cade's side, stabbing repeatedly in an attempt to distract him. The group rallied around Atlas, each member driven by desperation, by the fear of what would happen if they failed.

Cade's fury only seemed to grow, his monstrous frame absorbing their strikes with unnatural resilience. But Atlas's determination hardened. With a surge of adrenaline, he darted forward, unleashing a series of strikes aimed at Cade's neck and chest, hoping to weaken him enough for the final blow.

Cade roared, swinging wildly, but Atlas's movements were too swift, too calculated. With each swing of the katana, he chipped away at Cade's strength. Jax and Finn joined in, striking from the sides, diverting Cade's attention just long enough for Atlas to go in for another cut. Each swing of the blade was precise, unyielding, wearing Cade down piece by piece.

Finally, Atlas saw his opening. Cade stumbled, his massive form sagging under the combined attacks. With a roar of his own, Atlas swung the katana in a powerful arc, aiming for Cade's neck. The blade bit deep, severing Cade's head from his shoulders. Silence fell as Cade's body collapsed to the ground, but Atlas wasn't finished. Consumed by the rage of all they'd endured, he continued to hack at Cade's severed head, each swing a release of pent-up fury, grief, and exhaustion.

When he finally stopped, Cade's head lay in scattered pieces, unrecognizable, and Atlas stood over the remains, his breathing heavy, his body trembling. The adrenaline drained from him, and he staggered back, letting the katana drop to his side. Around him, his friends were similarly exhausted, sprawled on the floor, each of them worn out by the intensity of the battle.

The room was eerily quiet, the only sound the labored breathing of the survivors. They exchanged weary, dazed glances, each one processing the brutal reality of what they had just endured. Atlas looked down at his bloodstained hands, feeling the weight of the moment sink into his bones.

They had survived. But the cost was written in every cut, every bruise, every drop of blood spilled on the floor. And as they lay on the ground, their bodies and spirits exhausted, they knew that this fight was far from over.

CHAPTER XXXIV

In the Shadow of Goodbye

The group stood in the remains of the science tower, the silence oppressive. The once vibrant, safe space had become a graveyard for memories. Bloodstains still marked the floor where their friends—Alex and Taylor—had fallen, the echoes of their screams still ringing in the back of their minds. The weight of the loss sat heavily on them, a burden they weren't sure they could carry.

Atlas stood in the middle of the room, his chest tight with grief. He wasn't crying, didn't feel the tears that others might have expected. Instead, his gaze was hard, distant—focused on what had to be done. The fight with Cade had been brutal, and the scars of that battle were etched in the faces of everyone around him. But they had no choice. They had to keep moving forward. They couldn't let the past anchor them in place.

Jax, standing beside him, seemed just as steely. His usually bright and lively demeanor was now subdued, the loss of their friends weighing on him, but he wasn't the type to show weakness in front of the others. The mission had to continue.

Max was pacing back and forth, looking over the wreckage that had once been their refuge. His hands were steady, but his mind was elsewhere—haunted by what had happened, but more focused on the present. He had lost friends too. He had seen people torn apart in ways that seemed impossible, but now he had to stay sharp. They all did.

Finn, leaning against the wall, stared at the empty spot where Jess had fallen, her body still a memory in the back of his mind. Her screams, the way her body had contorted as Cade had bitten into her neck—it was burned into his soul. He had wanted to save her, to get to her before it was too late, but nothing had been able to stop the inevitability of her fate. The way she had bled out in his arms, struggling to speak, to tell him she was okay, but it was too late. She had died in his arms, and that would haunt him forever.

Chase walked over to Finn, his expression softening. "Finn, we've been through a lot. I know you're hurting. We all are. But we can't stay here. We need to get to Knox's camp."

Finn didn't answer immediately. He just shook his head, the grief making his chest tighten even more. He wanted to be angry—wanted to scream at the world for taking Jess from him. But instead, he stayed silent, unwilling to admit how close he was to falling apart.

"You don't have to do this alone," Chase continued, his voice low. "Let me drive the car. You need to focus, to rest."

Finn's eyes snapped to him, the edge of pain and anger sharpening his voice. "No, I'll drive. I can handle it. I need to handle it. I'm not... I'm not a damn liability."

Zane, who had been standing nearby, stepped forward with a concerned look on his face. "Finn, it's not about handling it. It's about surviving. We need you at your best, and if you're not there mentally, we all suffer."

"I said I can handle it," Finn repeated, his jaw set. "Just... leave me be."

The tension in the air was palpable, but there was no arguing with Finn's determination. Zane sighed, rubbing the back of his neck. "Alright, man. We'll do it your way. Just... don't make things harder on yourself."

Chase gave Zane a small nod, signaling him to step back. "We'll be alright. The mission's still on."

Max took a deep breath, his eyes scanning the others, then he stepped up and placed a hand on Finn's shoulder. "We're all hurting right now, but we have to keep going. We owe it to Jess, and to everyone else we've lost. No matter what happens, we keep moving forward. We need to get to Knox's camp, and that's our goal."

Atlas, who had been silently observing, now stepped in. He met Finn's eyes, his voice calm but firm. "We're leaving today. This doesn't end here, Finn. We get to Knox's camp, and we rebuild. For Jess. For everyone we lost. We have to keep going. And we will."

Finn nodded, swallowing hard, the weight of Atlas's words hitting him. As much as it hurt, he knew they were right. They had to keep going.

The decision had been made. The preparations were nearly complete. They had packed up what little they could carry, loading the essentials into both the helicopter and the explorer. The path ahead would be difficult, but they were ready.

Atlas, Jax, and Max would be taking the helicopter, the skies offering them a potential escape from the horrors that awaited them below. They could survey the area from above, clear the path of zombies as they went. The rest of the group would drive through the explorer, ensuring that the roads were safe and that everyone would have a way to escape if needed.

Before they left, Atlas looked around at the group. Everyone was silent, each lost in their own thoughts. He could feel their shared grief, the weight of the past pressing down on them. But they all knew what needed to be done.

Max slung his bag over his shoulder, giving Finn a brief, understanding glance before turning to the others. "Let's get this over with."

Jax looked at Atlas, his usual playful grin missing. "Ready to get the hell out of here?"

Atlas nodded, tightening his grip on his gear. "Let's do this."

The group made their way down to the vehicles. The helicopter sat ready on the terrace, its rotors still and waiting for the signal to take off. The explorer, packed and ready to go, was waiting on the ground floor.

As Atlas climbed into the helicopter with Jax, he looked back at the group gathered below. Finn was already in the driver's seat of the explorer, his hands tight on the wheel, his jaw set with determination. Zane climbed in beside him, and Chase took the passenger seat. The group was ready.

Before Atlas could give the signal, Finn's voice crackled through the comms. "You guys good up there?"

"We're good," Atlas replied, his voice steady. "We're about to take off. Just keep your eyes on the road, Finn."

"Yeah," Finn muttered. "I'm good. Let's get moving."

The engines roared to life, and the helicopter began its ascent, slowly lifting off the ground. Atlas watched as the campus grew smaller beneath them, the familiar view of the science tower fading as they gained altitude. Below, Finn drove the explorer slowly out of the campus grounds, his eyes scanning the road for any sign of danger.

The journey had begun. There was no turning back now.

As the group made their way through the streets, the helicopters soared high above, the wind whipping around them as they searched for any signs of zombies. The air felt heavy with the unspoken tension of what lay ahead.

It was a long road, one that would be filled with dangers, but for now, the group could only focus on the task at hand. They had one goal: get to Knox's camp. And so, they left behind the only place they had known as safe, the place that had once been their home, but was now just a memory. The campus was behind them, and the road ahead was uncertain. But they had to keep moving. The sun was setting as the group drove and flew, their destination looming ahead, uncertain and distant. There was no telling what lay ahead, but they had to try. They had to keep going. For Jess. For the lost. For the future they still hoped to build.

CHAPTER XXXV

In the Heart of The Shadows

The night had fallen heavy over the city, a cloak of darkness that seemed to smother everything beneath it. The group was on edge, moving through the streets in their two vehicles, the Explorer and the helicopter. Atlas, Jax, and Max flew above, eyes scanning the ground while Finn, Chase, and Zane navigated the roads below. It had been a day of intense tension, but as they neared the edge of the city, a strange kind of silence settled over them, broken only by the sound of their engines and the occasional growl of a distant zombie.

Finn's knuckles gripped the steering wheel, his eyes hollow from the loss of Jess. She had been his world, and now, every turn of the wheel, every bump on the road, reminded him of the harsh reality that she was gone. Still, he drove, the pain buried beneath layers of numbness. He couldn't let his grief consume him—not now. The group was depending on him.

Ahead, the flickering lights of the helicopter's search beams swept over the rooftops, illuminating the streets below. Max kept the gun trained on anything that moved, while Jax remained silent, his thoughts seemingly as distant as the horizon. Atlas, ever vigilant, was focused, the weight of their past days in the science tower weighing heavily on him. Each passing moment felt like a step toward the unknown, but they were moving forward—there was no other choice.

The streets were littered with wreckage from abandoned vehicles, overturned dumpsters, and the occasional skeletal remains of the uninfected. It wasn't quiet, not by a long shot. Zombies shuffled aimlessly through the streets, attracted by the sound of the vehicles. The headlights from the Explorer cut through the darkness, illuminating the eerie figures in the distance.

"Keep your eyes peeled," Atlas called over the radio, his voice sharp and commanding. "This is where the real challenge begins."

"We know," Jax replied, his voice laced with a hint of bitterness. The group's recent losses had left their morale shaken, but they still fought on. There was no room for weakness.

Suddenly, Finn slammed on the brakes. The screech of tires on asphalt filled the air as he jerked the wheel to the side. A cluster of zombies had appeared out of nowhere, their eyes glowing faintly in the dim light. The impact of their bodies against the front of the car sent a jolt through the group.

"They're everywhere!" Finn shouted, his breath coming fast. "We need to clear a path."

Atlas and Max, who were still circling above, dove down low, firing shots at the zombies below. Max's sharp eyes picked out targets with precision, picking off walkers one by one. Jax swung the helicopter into a wider circle, using the blades to push back the gathering horde and create space for the Explorer.

Finn and Zane, already on their feet, started unloading from the truck. Zane opened the rear door, pulling out a large rifle, while Finn grabbed a pair of machetes, his rage fueling every swing. The two of them cut through the zombies with a brutal efficiency that was almost mechanical, their bodies moving in perfect sync. The rest of the group did their part, shooting, clearing, and pushing back the relentless tide of the dead.

Max's voice crackled through the radio. "We've cleared the path ahead, but the streets are crawling with them. Get the car moving, now."

"Got it!" Finn yelled, slipping back into the driver's seat. His heart pounded in his chest, but he didn't hesitate. The engine roared to life as he floored the gas pedal, weaving through the streets, smashing through more zombies that stumbled into their way.

The helicopter remained above, keeping the zombies at bay. Atlas had to admit, there was something oddly comforting about having the bird's-eye view. The city, once a place of life, was now nothing more than a twisted maze of death. The headlights illuminated the carnage as they made their way down the streets, the silence that followed each kill deafening.

It didn't take long for them to encounter another group of zombies, larger this time. The groaning mass of flesh seemed endless, blocking their route to the outskirts of the city. Finn and Zane exchanged a look.

"Max, take them out," Atlas ordered. Max's response was immediate. The helicopter dove once more, taking advantage of the swarm's size. The gunfire rang out like thunder, cutting down zombies in swathes.

Finn drove with one hand, the other gripping the rifle by his side. He was done with trying to reason with the world. There was only survival. As the helicopter passed overhead, the last few zombies on their tail were shot down, but more were beginning to pour into the streets.

"Keep going," Atlas shouted. "We're almost out of here."

With another swipe of Finn's machete and a few more shots from Zane, the road ahead cleared. But the night was far from over. The group pressed forward, not knowing how much farther they had to go.

After a tense few minutes, the streets opened up into a desolate parking lot. The moon hung low in the sky, casting pale light over the empty space. The city's towering skyscrapers seemed to fade away in the distance, their outlines now shrouded in the blackness of the night. The group could see the edge of the city up ahead—an escape.

As they neared the outskirts, there was a momentary lull in the chaos. Finn slowed the car, his eyes scanning the horizon for any sign of movement. Jax's helicopter hovered above, keeping watch, while Max continued to fire down into the streets, picking off any remaining stragglers.

"We made it," Jax said, his voice almost a whisper.

But Atlas wasn't convinced. "We're not there yet."

The streets were now eerily quiet, almost too quiet. There were no more zombies in sight, but Atlas couldn't shake the feeling that something was wrong. They had cleared the city, but not without cost. Everyone had lost something in these past weeks, and the weight of that loss was never far from their minds. The sound of the helicopter blades kept the silence at bay, but even that wasn't enough to erase the tension that gripped them.

"Not yet," Atlas muttered. "But soon."

The journey through the city had taken its toll. Fatigue weighed on them, but the group still pressed on, determined to get through the night. The city was behind them now, but it still lingered in their minds, haunting them as they made their way toward the unknown.

As the first rays of dawn began to break on the horizon, the city finally slipped from view, swallowed by the darkness of the night. They were close to the outskirts now, just one more day away from Knox's camp, the promised sanctuary where they hoped to find safety.

But even as the light began to return, it felt more like a fleeting illusion. They had fought through the darkness, and now they would face whatever lay ahead.

The group was exhausted, their bodies and spirits worn thin. Yet, they still had a goal to reach. Atlas glanced at the others, feeling the weight of their shared struggle. They had survived the night, but tomorrow would be the true test.

With one last look at the city behind them, Atlas pushed forward. Their journey was almost over

CHAPTER XXXVI

Shadows of the Awakening

The journey had been long, exhausting, and riddled with moments of uncertainty, but now, at last, they had reached the place they had been striving toward: Knox's camp. The sun hung low in the sky, casting a golden light over the horizon. The landscape had transformed from urban chaos to open fields, the once-terrifying city now a distant memory.

Ahead, nestled between rolling hills, stood a massive fortress—Dawnhaven—its towering walls stretching high into the sky. The imposing gates of the fortress loomed like a silent sentinel, the heavy stone walls darkened with age and the weight of survival. It was a place built for protection, a place of refuge. But more than that, it was a symbol of everything they had fought for, everything they had lost. This was where they hoped to find some semblance of peace.

Atlas's heart pounded in his chest as he piloted the helicopter toward the entrance, the rest of the group following closely behind in the Explorer. His mind was racing, but there was also a sense of cautious relief. After everything they had endured, they had finally made it. Yet, despite the sense of accomplishment, something gnawed at the back of his mind. He knew all too well that peace was fleeting in a world like this.

The gates of Dawnhaven creaked open slowly, revealing a long road that led to the heart of the fortress. The walls were thick, reinforced with metal and stone, and there were watchtowers at every corner, manned by armed survivors.

There were other vehicles parked along the side of the road, some clearly abandoned, others neatly lined up as if preparing for a new arrival. The place felt like a world unto itself, a self-contained existence that had somehow managed to survive the worst of the apocalypse.

As the helicopter and Explorer rolled toward the gates, Atlas could see figures moving on the walls, the watchful eyes of the survivors observing them. It was strange to be this close to something resembling normalcy. The group had spent so long fighting for their survival that the idea of settling down, of finding a place to call home again, felt almost alien.

The gates fully opened, revealing Knox himself standing at the entrance, arms crossed, waiting. His once-dapper appearance had shifted over time, his clothes now more rugged, his hair longer, but the look in his eyes remained the same—calculating, a little distant, but undeniably relieved to see them. He had been a friend once, and now he was the leader of a thriving camp.

Atlas stepped out of the helicopter first, his boots hitting the gravel with a heavy thud. He squared his shoulders, instinctively adjusting the strap of his weapon. The rest of the group followed behind him, stepping into the safety of the camp, their eyes scanning their surroundings. Even in the face of sanctuary, there was a subtle wariness that hung in the air.

Max and Jax, the two most cautious of the group, remained near the Explorer, their eyes darting toward the walls and the people watching from above. Finn, still reeling from Jess's death, walked with a heavy heart, his gaze focused on the ground, his face drawn with grief. Zane and Chase exchanged quiet words, perhaps discussing the best course of action for the coming days.

Knox's attention was fixed on Atlas, his old friend, a faint grin curling on his lips.

"We're here, Knox," Atlas said, his voice flat but resolute.

Knox nodded. "Safe as it gets in this world. We've got supplies, walls, and people who know how to fight. But don't get comfortable just yet. We've been attacked a few times. Zombies get smarter, harder to kill." He paused. "But we've got everything under control for now. You've done well to get here."

The gates closed behind them with a finality that made Atlas's chest tighten. There was no going back now.

As they moved deeper into the camp, Atlas's mind wandered back to the people he had lost. His thoughts drifted to Jess, to Cade, to the countless others who had fallen along the way. The pain was fresh, and yet there was also something else—an awareness that he had to keep moving forward. The group needed him, and he needed to be strong for them.

And then, as they walked past a row of tents, Atlas's thoughts wandered to someone else. Hope. He couldn't shake the image of her face from his mind. He had no idea where she was, if she was still alive, or if he would ever see her again.

But somehow, he couldn't bring himself to give up hope. Not yet. Because he believed—

Hope can be the one thing that can save a person or Hope can become the one thing that can lead to his destruction.

He sighed, feeling the weight of the world pressing down on his chest.

And then, the scene shifted.

The group stood near the main courtyard inside Dawnhaven, the dying sun casting molten streaks across the stone. A quiet, eerie stillness blanketed the camp. But their attention wasn't on the fires or the survivors bustling about—it was on Atlas.

He had stepped away.

Just a few feet—but it was enough to make it feel like miles. He stood alone at the edge of the inner gate, his back to them, gazing out at the wasteland they had left behind. The shadows stretched long around him, swallowing his frame in the growing dark.

Knox stood beside the others, silent, arms crossed tightly. The tension between them all was no longer subtle—it was palpable.

Unspoken accusations lingered in the air.

Someone had died—one of their own. And Atlas hadn't hesitated.

Could a man kill the very thing he swore to protect—and still call himself their savior?

Atlas had led them through hell. But in doing so... what had he become?

Had the monster Atlas became to protect them... turned against them?

Atlas turned slowly, his face half-shrouded in the dusk. His eyes met theirs.

And then, his lips curled into a smile.

Not of reunion. But of something else. Something colder. Darker.

A grimful, devilish smile that made their blood run cold.

He took one step closer, the weight of the world on his shoulders—and none in his eyes.

"Everything we've endured... the chaos, the bloodshed, the nightmares—they were just the beginning," Atlas said, his voice steady but laced with a dark edge. He took a slow breath, eyes narrowing as a grim smile changed into a more feral one across his face. "That was merely the Awakening."

He paused, letting the weight of his words settle.

"But this... this is the Fortress of the Undead."

And the shadows swallowed the rest.